THE LOST POET
OF WOODLAWN

by S. Sullivan

with an introduction by Shaun Vain

THE
Lost Poet
of Woodlawn
by
Shaun Michael Vain

The Lost Poet of Woodlawn with introduction by Shaun Vain.

For more information regarding this publication and to order copies, contact the author by way of the publisher. Send packages to S. Vain % Future Publishing Service. At the time of this printing, you may find information about ways to contact Future Publishing Service by visiting www.thelostpoetry.com, or you may conduct an investigation as to find the best way to contact us.

If you wish to contact the author by mail, include a self-addressed envelope with postage if you expect a reply to your query. You may receive a response, but there's no guarantee.

ISBN: 978-0-578-53353-7

10 9 8 7 6   FPS   e 4 3 2 1   06 22   23 22 21 20 19
First edition. Paperback.

This book is a work of fiction. All characters, including its author, are a creation of S. Vain. Any similarities to persons living, dead, or imaginary are coincidental.

Note about production: The body of this book is typed using Garamond, named after Parisian engraver Claude Garamond.

Featuring

THE "LOST" POET

. . . and even stranger characters

narrating a splendid story of self discovery

To future poets,
may you always find the right words.

And to my future wife,
if she'll have me
after I wrote this,
this that wrote me too.

S. Vain
4/30/2019

.... INTRODUCTION ....

Last winter, I met with an old friend from high school that I hadn't seen in ages. I had been meaning to find out what they were up to, but I hadn't made the time until they found out some terrible news about an illness in their family, so I thought it was best to hurry up and cheer them up. I was waiting for them outside a café when something caught my eye in the antique shop across the way. *Jumpin' Saturday's* always had the least interesting items in their window, like the old, perfect vases and white dishes. They were in the habit of always selling those beautiful antiques that people buy to impress party guests, so I usually don't think the store is worth my time. That was until I saw, in their window, an interesting item to add to my next presentation of rare artifacts.

The relic, henceforth it shall be known, was beside my favorite toy from childhood that was preserved in mint condition.

The sleek style of my favorite action hero was modeled perfectly in a collectable toy that was never to be opened. I briefly thought about purchasing it, and releasing it unto the world, but I figured I was an adult, so I should buy adult things. Even if I had the extra money to splurge, none of those vases would have ever interested me. I took a look through the comic books, but I still felt guilty for buying childish things. That's when I returned to the hero in the window, and the shopkeeper said to me, with a tone of urgent salience, "You'll be a hero one day! I know it."

I looked at the book in the display to see it was a bound journal marked with an imprint that reads, "Heroic Tales". The unusual book appealed to my sense of mysticism, and I saw it to be a candidate for my next presentation. My mission from then on was to convince everyone that I had come upon the perfect item that surveys the human spirit, starting with my friendly reunion.

Before I left the collectables emporium, I tried rifling through a crate filled with exquisite reproductions of journals that a popular artist kept throughout their travels in foreign countries. Organized perfectly to allow one to select from snapshots of life in other parts of the world, there were slides from the artist's journey through Switzerland, Italy, France, and other parts of Europe. I bought a few of the journals because I recognized the artist and thought they would go nicely in my catalogue of rare books and other artifacts, which I frequently present in public venues.

I left to go meet my friend for coffee. To help my friend find some cheer, I showed him the rare artist books that I had found. My friend liked the new specimens in my catalogue very much, so much so that I decided to show him the rare relic I purchased from the window display. Even though there wasn't an author listed on the relic, I thought that *Heroic Tales* would hold up to his inspection. The relic kept his attention immediately, even more than the popular artist's journals. It was in a formulaic, stylized script of cursive handwriting. Pages upon pages of text were filled with mysterious entries.

My friend speculated that the relic was an artifact left behind by a great writer. We took turns reading its pages aloud, happily, smiling whenever one of us felt like we were right there with their group. Upon showcasing and presenting some of the strange work I had just found to my friend, I found myself utterly enchanted by the author's words.

"We surveyed the area for clues from lost civilizations," I read from the relic, "but what we found was something less expected. A great mine of clues for the future of mankind was ours to share with the world."

"How strange," said my friend. "Where does it say that?" I showed him the text, and I continued, reading, "While drifting among the sensual rock, and the glaciar formations with colors that only the soul of nature may spring forth, it is to our astonishment and delight to present these precious jewels of enchantment." I turned a page and continued reading from the strange relic notebook in my possession. Without lingering, I read aloud the next two pages, as shown in the depiction on the following page.

When I finished reading those two pages, I turned to the next page, and there I became languid in my recitation of the author's penmanship. Truthfully, I had trouble understanding what the author was trying to convey. Eventually, I showed it to my friend, and he told me it looked like a map of his ancestral province. Despite being a dilettante archeologist, particularly in gathering resources for my

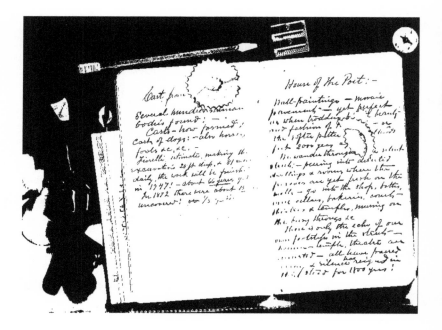

presentations, I have acquired but an acute knowledge of geography. "I thought that was a splotch of coffee I spilled," I jostled my friend, but I sincerely had trouble reading the names of the cities on the paper. "I would have had to look at an atlas for hours, but my proud companion, I thank thee," I admitted after further observations.

As if we were thrown from the glacial chasms ourselves, we found yet an immediate shift into conversation about our own lives. He spent only a moment telling me about his kinfolk troubles before asking me about how my life was compared to when we last saw each other. At that very moment, I realized I hadn't done anything meaningful with my life since we last spoke. All of the people who were in my circle then have gone on to medical school and scholarly research, or design and engineering modern marvels of human ingenuity, but I was simply a curator of lost works.

All of my years I've spent learning about the world, yet I have never left the safety of the familiar nest. The only time I did anything worth mentioning was when I left everything I owned to join the circus, and I became a professional juggler, but I can't keep juggling and showcasing oddities all my life, can I? In that moment I felt I needed to do something worthy for the world, so I vowed, to my friend that day, to follow the clues left in the incredible relic that I had but recently discovered.

That's when my own story of adventure began, and since its throws first started I haven't had the time to write about it, certainly not enough to get into a worthwhile discussion here. Though I hadn't deciphered the name of the author of the relic that guided us to 'The Lost Poet of Woodlawn', I felt confident following the author's instructions because they were so detailed in their pursuit, archiving hundreds of photographs to assist us along our journey. They were for sale at *Jumpin Saturday's* in a catalogue of glass slides.

Of further interest to you might be the various treasures that have been unearthed around the globe, that have produced similar finds as the relic that brought us to Sullivan's book. Any substantial discoveries must remain in the hands of an entrusted company or individual, like national government humanitarian foundations or a trustworthy historian. Often I am able to arrange for the care of historic treasures in public museums for the people to witness, but I am always able to photograph and write about such findings.

On the particular finding you have in your hands, I was incredibly lucky, for, as you can see, this particular treasure is easily replicated for distribution. Although Shane Sullivan's family has asked that they not be contacted, I have already answered many questions on their behalf, questions pertaining to this conquest of human evolution. It is my hope that I have done right in presenting the treasure that this relic helped me ascertain. My intention behind this brief introduction was to answer any questions that might be lingering before the text is presented in its entirety. However, if I may have raised more queries, take heed: it is not my intention to be dissected.

When I first showed my friend the map of his familial country, I was shocked and delighted that he advised me to visit and follow the directions laid before me. He has a history of being hesitant when presented with new ideas. He often forgets, there were times when he has had to find courage to take risks for himself, and how he overcame his anxiety to get in front of a crowd to tell his first jokes at a public library is noteworthy enough. For, nowadays, he tells complicated anecdotal jokes in front of large crowds of ticketed patrons.

Though he didn't concede entirely, he quickly agreed that taking risks is necessary if one is to make one's worth. "If you're going to get over mopping up floors after your own lectures about strange gems and shark teeth, you'll need to take risks like this one. You've paid your dues."

"I have more to pay," I assured him. "I'll pay them all the ways I can along the way to be sure that I'm living honourably."

Upon my friend's concession, we took one of the entries and followed the course set by the author of the relic. I was intrigued by an entry in the book that directed us to the House of the Poet. I kept steady the course of our journey, which was not entirely graceful. I hope to present the events of our harrowing tale one day when the time is right and when I have time to actually write it all down, of course. In short, it was a long journey, over icy mountains and through decrepit caverns; we had to risk our lives far more than I care to admit. I'll go into detail at some point, I suppose. For now, it's safe to say that it was worth every worry and fear along the way to get to behold the specimen you see here.

When we reached the gate outside of the House of the Poet, we followed the directions precisely, and upon the tumultuous end of our journey, "It goes to show you that perseverance is part of the path," I said to him, aware of the stench of greed brimming beneath my breath. I grinned to the thought of treasures to sell and empires to examine in front of applauding crowds of aristocrats. My mind was drunk on applause.

"I tried to point you away from missing the point," said my friend. "You can find these types of artifacts all over, but you'd be better off not wasting your time making them yourself." My friend revealed that he had planted the treasure map in the antique shop for me to find. "At least it goes to show you that you make good company," he said. He visited his sick relative, and I went with him, begrudgingly. When we left his family's domicile, I went back by myself to the House of the Poet to examine the grounds, and I was not met with disappointment. Indeed, I was met with this book, one stranger than any other I had found in all my trepidations.

Even after finding the mystical book that may have manifested out of the ether, my friend still thought it was his civic duty to try and persuade me to pursue a more stable career. But I'll venture forth with my wits about me anyhow. I'll certainly venture my dreams through something more stable and sure when I create a work of mine own, but for now you are left with the 'found text' you have before you.

'The Lost Poet of Woodlawn' was created with authenticity unmatched by the fake relic drawn up by my friend. In its original form, the artifact has been proven as a work that is certain to be written in the future, and somehow it is proven that the work will divinely be brought backwards to our time for me to find in that sacred place that I found it.

Using new algorithms and untested equipment, scientists have concluded the source material to be from a time just before the end of the twenty-first-century. The process used was an augmentation of the traditional carbon-14 dating procedure used to represent a growth in the radioactive carbon-14. The decay of this, I am told, is normally close to a half-life of six millennia. The text uncovered for you today was written on paper showing a *growth* of the radioactive carbon. As my colleagues will concur, its information could readily help humanity find its way to a better tomorrow, for so it appears such a lot is the poet's intention.

Upon trespassing, I dared to unlock an etheric case that presented itself to me, and I have sworn to present its contents unaltered, in their entirety. A note at the bottom of the strange plastic chasm I unlocked seemed to have appeared from out of the ether as well, as it contains a description of the author of these works. The poet is named Shane Sullivan. From what we've been able to deduce through investigating Sullivan's writings, he's the author of a body of poetry to be called 'The Hedges', which I surmise to be of some great significance.

With great alacrity, myself and others at Future Publishing Service took to deciphering the poet's writing: his cursive letters were difficult to understand and required thorough analysis. His strange diction and the way he spells certain words may be suggestions of the evolution of English language, so I've taken careful liberty to preserve them for this edition. The whimsical journey of the poet from

Woodlawn tells the story of a young man responsible for crafting 'The Hedges'. The story of his has slipped from the ether to be presented here.

Squire V. *(Copenhagen, Denmark)* Nov. 10, 2016

In A Place Where . . .

. . . the purification of the atmosphere, reorders the molecular construction of air . . .

. . . machines farm and fly for the benefit of humanity.

They create an arrangement of the perfect composition of properly charged particles, recycling and organizing the Earth . . . and the ether.

Such brilliant compositions of particles are possible when humankind stops stalling the process, but for centuries human beings have been rivaling their own creations. We put them out of work in the fields when a horse was better for plowing, put them out of work in the factories, too, when the looms worked better than tiny, nimble hands and fingers.

. . . The rivalry between the working class and the machines has nearly come to an end, for a breakthrough in evenly distributing wealth accompanies rising technology. Automation has finally taken up the majority of less desired service jobs, so work is a leisurely activity. For, mostly every individual given the choice to live off of the wealth of our domain over the Earth and the machine have chosen to feed themselves fully.

Only a select few live with intolerance of limitless abundance, and prosperity is seldom questioned and thwarted by those who aim to end humankind's relation with its creation.

"Sultan of Cadab tricked his soldiers, burrying their vestments beneath the mines o' Adab! To there you may find each in vaulted worldly treasure near town'o Dabra, but, do go alone, for: worldly vestment many, no spirit sum. Misty Abra, take this warning or die trying to split the lot between too many! As Braca the Grate[†] when others did die undermine, left his lot, course set for Raca."

-A passage from Heroic Tales

[†]Fifth century sailor and knight known by many as Braca the Grateful

— *"De-tecting atmospheric concentration. YIP! Excessive levels of nitrogren. BOP!"*

. . . .

— *"Transference formula discovered. Synthesizing elemental formula. Synthesizing."*

. . . .

— *"VAROOM! Etheric embodiment processing. Process complete. Analyzing. Atmospheric concentration detected. Concentration neutralized. Moving to next air pocket. Detecting concentration."*

. . . .

. . .

The Lost Poet of Woodlawn

. . .

PROLOGUE

"KEEP MY NAME OUT OF IT," I said to my son when he told me what he was writing, and he agreed to never put my name in his work. He carefully left my name and my adopted surname out of the story that he felt he had to tell to the world. For a good reason, he put it in print and not available through digital screens. Except in short excerpts, the entire novel you hold in your hands is only bound by paper, yet there are some copies that have been circulating on the internet, of course, but nothing official has been published from Shane Sullivan through digital means, and nothing ever will. For, unlike his poetry, it is the nature of his prose to not take flight on the digital devices we all have close by.

Shane wanted to be in print after all the poems he wrote have been displayed on devices around the planet. There's no telling how many people have read his poetry and been infected by his words. The rich, crisp quality of paper is something different. There's pride in having a work in print. The words that become imprinted on paper have a tendency to stay around longer. There's certainly a great service that many writers do by having their books available as digitally formatted e-books: the books are easier for anyone to pick up without visiting a bookstore, and there's less paper being used to get their ideas out there. However, this is not the typical book to be read.

The reader will take note of the quality of the poet that speaks about subjects that have a certain mysterious form surrounding them. The ether is particularly puzzling to most of us

2

non-dead people, which make up most of the readers, I suppose. The words used to describe a place that is not easy to grasp should be captured on paper, rather than thrown about without regard in the digital world. This is because the ether does not want to be forgotten. There was a sort of unspoken agreement that my son, the poet, had to take in order to write about the ether and such elements of nature. As he has described to me, the stench of death would linger upon him if he were to send his words out to devices across the planet. The words would move too quickly, and they would take a new shape that could be catastrophic! I'm not quite sure what that shape would be, and I couldn't get my son to elaborate more upon the point, but he seemed forever stuck in the way he felt, so I left it be. I believe the line from this book that best sum'rizes this point sufficiently and precisely is as follows:

> *"Every drop of ink is a letter imprinted on time that I cannot return, and it moves like the river has rushed, with or without me in it."*

. . . .

But I digress from the reason which I am here in words to write about the book you hold in your hands today. Writing isn't my chosen profession. My son fits well in the field, but I work with images more than letters, and I hold a treasure trove of what I have made that will line the walls of palaces for years after my death, I am told by Shane. He took his poetic spirit from my dear aunt, as expressed in the first chapter. I believe that's where he got it, for the other writer in our family, Lynch, is a coward who crawled off to live in a rut and deliver letters that no one ever asked for.

My birth-father never had a way with words as I remember him when I was a child. He sent a card to me on my birthday, after he left us, years after, and all he did was put his name, without "Love,". How am I to believe he had a single metaphor in his brain? Surely, he had suffered like an artist. To have left those he loved to start a new life as a postman in another town. He left everything he *said* that he loved anyhow. That might be what poetry does to us. It's a grand lie we put on in our minds. I truly hope that my son turns out different, so I must say I don't see my birth-father, Lynch, to be a poet.

The reason I am brought in to help introduce 'The Lost Poet of Woodlawn' isn't because I have a way with words, and it's not because I have a kinship to the author. I'm brought in to help introduce this work because I saved the author's work from being taken to the scrap yard on a one-way trip to Junktown. I mean to say, Shane's work was being siphoned from him without his knowledge, and I was the one to pull the plug on that operation. Listen how:

Shane was fifteen when he received a strange package in the mail. He had never received a single gift from my birth-father, but Lynch sent him a birthday present that year. I thought it was sweet that he had finally recognized his grandson with a gift. It wasn't much, but it might've been all he could afford, I thought to myself at the time. It was a die cast model of the ship used in one of the sci-fi movies that was popular at the time. Shane had loved the movies, and I even got him listening to classical music when I bought him the soundtrack to the movie. I thought Lynch must have taken a guess at what the boy would like, and he was right on the money with his gift.

4

The model sat on my son's shelf to collect dust like those sorts of things do. I told him we would get a plastic case to house it, but I didn't rush to get it for him. I was preoccupied with stained glass at the time. I have a collection of stained glass pieces nowadays that catch the light perfectly as it shines into my sitting room. Shane went back to his writings with a new sense of purpose. He felt charged with the recognition of being alive that he had always deserved. Every boy likes to be recognized by his elders, especially those that have been estranged. It was a simple gesture, but I thought it was deeply kind.

Soon, I would find out that the gesture was riddled with regret. For, I noticed something eerie about the simple model. While my son hadn't had much experience in acting on stage or on film, the budding poet did like to read his work aloud when he was through with it. Even as a teen, he was reading poetry at full volume in his bedroom to an audience of close friends, or a line of action figures. He didn't care who was listening. That's the way many writers work, I am told. They need to hear the words to verify that they are worth reading again. At age fifteen, Shane was working on an epic poem about growing up that only an adolescent boy could have concocted. It wasn't the best thing I'd heard, but it was unique to a boy's youthful experience in our times. It was kind of vulgar to be honest, so I told him my reaction to it. While I was talking to him, I glanced at the shelf that held the model Lynch gifted him, and I heard the strangest thing. The model on the shelf was making the sound of gears grinding within it.

Sure enough, I picked up the simple model, and with a screwdriver, I pried it open to look at its inner-mechanism. I found that it wasn't the simple model I thought it was, but it was a sneaky device used to listen in on what my son was saying. The gift sent from Lynch wasn't a toy for a boy, it was a device he was using to listen to what my son was writing, and he was putting those words out under his own name.

This is why I am here to present Shane's work to you today. He felt that I would know best what should be heard by the rest of the world, and if I do not present it, I fear someone like Lynch will pick it up to give it to others in a form that is untrue to its origin.

I caught that wicked man, and eventually Shane thought it made sense to release these notes and the story behind our strange existence.

A.S.   July 11, 20—

PART ONE:

"IF ONLY THE POET COULD SEE,"

ONE

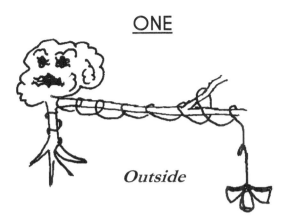

Outside

I've never seen someone so helplessly bound as my great aunt was when I last visited her. She was tired of the retirement home they put her in, so she went to live with her daughter and my mother, in Woodlawn Manor. Woodlawn is a town on the Eastern Seaboard, almost immediately south of the Mason Dixon Line.

"There's something you should know since you're taking up words. Like your grandfather."

"I didn't know Hank was good with words."

"Who? Hank? Oh, him. He, I don't know about, but your mother's real father was inspired to be a poet, you know. He's very well known. He traveled overseas to write about fishing in villages near the Cook Islands. He was writing for a sports journal when he started writing poetry. . . . He's very well known, and he gave the islanders such fine silk Hawaiian shirts. I remember reading his letters he sent your mother."

"He sent letters?"

"Sure. He tried to keep in touch, and he tried to keep being her father."

"But then he quit trying."

"The native Maori People showed him their secret fishing holes. They imparted their wisdom too, that he would cause less pain if he left her be. They were happy with the silk shirts, I suppose. They didn't have anything like that there."

"No, I bet they were happy to have him around. I bet he was happy to be there. While my mother had to worry where her next meal was coming from."

"Hank showed up early on. He provided us with the Manor, you know. He'll be missed dear. But you shouldn't burn your bridges with your grandfather yet, sweetheart, since your grandfather—"

"Lynch. His name is Lynch."

"Lynch had this aunt who inspired him, before he picked up from his obligations and left to get fat on the world's pleasures. His aunt was a school teacher, one of the first women superintendents in fact. But most of all, she was a poetess."

"Really."

"She had a book with all her poetries in it. She wrote and wrote. All those poetries were lost forever. She died, and Hank bought Woodlawn Manor at auction. That's when he met Fifi."

"And they lived happily ever after. I know the story, but your nephew left out without leaving a trace, and they say we look a lot alike."

"You do look alike, and you both have that poetic sensibility. Yes. But you aren't a trickster like he."

Blue-splotches covered her hands that trembled wildly, as she searched for a book to show me. The poem she held out to me was written with crisp, cursive letters:

10

To the Future . . .

To the future poet
(who finds this book),
you mightn't know it,
but thoughts do hook
in people's minds,
in dreams they make
real world sublime,
and fears they break

before impacting time,
'tween poetic & fact.

so don't fear
coloured sound
dripping of tear
feelings abound
capturing life
Reflecting charm
Sharpen your knife
Slaughter the farm
of a rhyming scheme
homegrown poem regime.

Oh, future poet I'll never meet,
stringing words better, newer than me,

11

Raise clean scrolls from ash without defeat.
Bring to all what you've been raised to be.
For, the whole world doesn't know it,
but we raised you for greatness, my dear.
Though the world doesn't know yet, the poet
will fight with ink to make it better here.
So noble poet, you know now,
it matters; you just don't know how.

. . . .

That poetry pushed me forth from Woodlawn, and now I stand outside and bang on the door until an old haggardly woman comes to answer my calls. I ask her who she is and tell her who I am. I tell her how I am looking for the man who left my mother to grow up without a father.

"You shouldn't be here," she says. She shuts the door quickly and cautiously. I don't move. I stand in that spot by the door on the wicker welcome mat that is muddy and shredded.

Eventually the haggardly old woman must have felt sorry for me. She offers me a coffee but I decline the gesture.

"Your grandfather—"

"Lynch."

"Yes," she agrees with my correction, for names like mother and grandfather mean more than biology.

Lynch doesn't earn the title. The man who adopted my mother and her sister when they were children, however, does earn it. He wasn't the best dad at first, as I was told, but he grew up into one anyway. His name was Hank, and he was a truck driver from Dundalk, Maryland.

Hank smoked, but never drank alcohol while I knew him. But he had stories he'd tell me when I was a boy. He would drink when he was a young man. He and his friends would "get loaded." They'd push the glass bottles into the dirt on the hill where they would drink.

"Before the summer of my eighteenth birthday was over, glass bottles lined the entire hillside." He never touched alcohol much when he got older though. I think sometime after his mother passed away he gave it up altogether. He must have wanted to honor her death by raising his standards with a more conscious approach to living. And around then is when he became a good grandfather, too.

Hank taught me to drive after he taught my mother, my aunt, my uncle, even my great aunt, who got her license late in life. He taught me how to hang drywall as well. I'd be lying if I said either skill ever really came in handy, but I'm grateful for those types of things I did learn from Hank.

His mother spoke Italian, not English. The old Sicilian woman died when I was only five or so, but she was there when I first woke up to the world. My very first memory was with Ma Vito. She sat in a rocking chair and knitted while I played with my yellow metal Tonka trucks in front of the fish tank in our sitting room at the Manor. The dump truck had unloaded Matchbox Cars, and the bulldozer dropped its scoop with the touch of the black metal lever, when a great big oscar fish jumped from the tank in the living room. She kept on rocking while I ran to the other room to tell my mother and my grandmother. They were gabbing around the kitchen table, and neither one of them would quit flapping at their lips long enough to listen to me tell them about the fish that was flopping around on the carpet.

When they finally stopped talking neither one of them would believe the things that came from my tiny mouth. The old Sicilian woman saw the fish jump from the tank. She believed me.

My mother always warned me about alcohol and how my father drank often, fearing that I might like the drink just the same as he. She got a little carried away . . . telling me not to let the booze carry me away.

"That liquid devil will take you underwater with it, and you'll drown yourself in sin if you're not careful, son," she'd say often. I knew she was acting out of love, and resentment, towards my father. I love my father but I don't take after him like that.

Another thing I learned growing up is that women take after their father's mother, and men take after their mother's father. Unfortunately, my mother's father left when she was young, too young for her to remember him. My point being I have never met my mother's father to tell whether or not we're alike.

So here I stand. I am defiant. The woman who offers me coffee sees I'm not moving. She can tell I'm not going to leave. I'm not going anywhere. She unrolls her sleeves and unwrinkles her jowls to smile slightly.

"You can wait inside," she offers. "Lynch will be a few hours. He's finishing his rounds nearby. And he's still got to take the mail truck back to the shop. You know you should have warned us you'd be stopping by. Coming in unannounced is how you get yourself shot."

"That would have been a story for your grandchildren if you have any," I tell her.

"We had better things to do," she says.

I sit on the porch near a nicely groomed privet. I swing and swing.

TWO

Loose Screws and Italian Opera

Hi ho, in tunnel we burrow,
Hi ho!
Dig, claw to better tomorrow.
"Hi ho!" exclaims the Hedgehog.
"Hi ho!"

—*The Hedges*, issue no. 1

People often ask me where the idea for writing 'The Hedges' came from. This might not surprise anybody today. To hear that a working class son of Italian immigrants had a vividly troubling upbringing that made him into a tough as nails type of guy. He never spit, but he smoked and cussed if he happened to be alone, or in the company of ruffians. Hank was once a young boy who was coddled by his parents. His mother would make two steaks, one for her and one for him. At dinner, he'd eat both of them, so he grew up to be round and tough like well-done rib-eye.

When Hank first got around to getting to know me, I was just a boy, so I wasn't worth much to him yet. I was still a walking, talking foot massager and back-scratcher-holder. If you wanted to get a present for Hank, you either got him something he could use on the road, or you got him a movie he could watch when he got home from driving truck. For most men the go-to gift is usually a wallet or tie, but not for the hardworking guy that Hank was. In fact, he'd laugh if anyone actually gave him a tie. I remember his reaction after I bought a wallet for the man from the school bookstore:

"Shane, I can get that at a truck stop. Why'd you spend all your money?"

"It's not all my money," I'd say.

"Oh! You must be rich," he'd say, and he'd usually say something to the effect of, "Better to be born rich. I wish I was born rich instead of so good looking."

I grew taller, almost the tallest in my class in fact. As I got closer to the ceiling, I suppose some intrinsic bell went off in the old man's head. His noggin started thinking that I was strong enough to hold sheets of drywall over my head while he hurried up to secure them to the ceiling with screws. He'd tighten them first with his gun, but the battery would run out, so he'd have to hurry up to find another battery. Or else he'd have to secure it to the ceiling by hand, with a screwdriver. We bought the thinnest drywall we could find at one-quarter inch or less, I believe, but no matter the weight I couldn't hold up the damn sheets all day, not while he fumbled around.

Eventually, we wisened up on our approach. When I showed him I could measure and count higher than he thought I could, he saw an even better use for his back-scratcher-holder. Using my calculations, we built a rig after measuring the height of the ceiling we were replacing. It was a simple rig composed of a few two-by-fours nailed together. But it was sturdy and took some of the pressure off my arms and back.

When I put the rig in commission I noticed he was still scrambling with the drill. He didn't realize I was watching him. I was studying how the old man solved problems. I watched how he moved, and I saw how he crafted along the way.

17

As Hank was making a design in the wood with a miter saw, the drywall stayed pressed against the ceiling.

"Just another minute. Can you hold it up still?"

"Yeah," I said.

"Your arms aren't hurting you?" he asked. His questioning the fatigue of my arms indicated to me that he must have forgotten all about the device we constructed earlier. I figured that it was perhaps a mental slip since his mind was getting older. He sang some classic country ballad, and he ordered the sheet to be held higher.

He wasn't paying attention as he mitered. He cut his finger and shouted, "Damn it! Oh that hurt so bad." His diabetic blood quickly congealed over the wound with a thick glob that must have been moving around inside his veins somehow, but when he sprung a leak that glob fell right in place.

His mitering culminated in circles along the tops of the woodwork along the windows in the sitting room of the Woodlawn Manor. "What fine Italian craftsmanship," I recently told my grandmother about the woodwork.

"The roof needs work, but I can't afford to fix it," Fifi told me when I made the comment. I agreed that the ceiling looked like it was ready to cave in, but I was not the man to fix it by myself.

He finished with the sawing, he vacuumed up the dust, and he painted the wood with a white primer when the dust had settled.

He must have forgot I was there. As he painted he started to sing. I'd heard my grandfather sing all types of songs, I'd thought. Up until that point I'd heard his windpipes play operatic country songs that gave me desires to write a ballad of that type, but my voice was scratchy so I never sang, unless a rock song came on while we were working. He sang some classic rock too, and classic folk, like Jim

Croce, whom he admired and wished were still alive. This day was different than most, for he wasn't harping along with *Bad, Bad Leroy Brown*, nor was he singing something from George Straight, or any other of his usual picks. He was singing . . . in the Italian language.

Hank's parents were from Sicily, and neither of them spoke English. I had thought that he had completely neglected to learn to speak his parents' native tongue. For, I once asked him about his heritage, and he said he despised all the Italians just the same as all the other races, "except for the Native Americans because we put them through hell." At a young age, I gathered that anyone who was put through hell deserved some sympathy and understanding at least. But he didn't think much of being Italian, so despite any racial bias he gave off, he usually came off as humble.

There he was though! Singing an Italian opera with a paint brush as a microphone. White paint splattered everywhere. I'd already given up on the drywall. I lowered the sheet to the ground, and moved the two-by-four brace out of the way.

I was quiet, so I was able to observe him closely. But I wasn't the most coordinated boy, so I fell back some, but instead of falling to the carpeted floors of the Manor, I landed there with Hank in Dundalk.

If you've been to Maryland's cities and cities around the Eastern Seaboard, surely you're familiar with places like Dundalk. For its population of homogenous, friendly people wanting fast thrills, Dundalk is Maryland's version of a popular crowded slum. Like Jersey City was when it was close to New York, before the fault appeared and continents drifted apart. Dundalk is that close to Baltimore

City. It gets a bad reputation for its lack of diversity and lower class mentality. But I found myself in simpler times.

He was a happy young boy, not much younger than I was at that time. I'll never forget how I saw the way in which Hank emulated his father. His dad was putting silver dollars onto the bottoms of tiny horse feet. It was his trademark. His father was Peter Vito, owner of Vito's Miniature Horse Stable and Saloon. I saw Hank run around the stable door with energy I'd never seen in him before, he ducked under the gate to let Peter inside, and Peter showed his customers around the tiny ponies.

They carefully selected a horse and paid the man. Peter combed the horse's mane one last time, and he patted it on the head. Behind them were mounds of manure that they tried to ignore, and a plaque on the wall may have helped: "He who steps upon his own mound of misery will stand higher than those around him."

That's when Hank saddled up the horse. He hopped onto its back and rode it out of the stable. The customers inquired about the young man, but Peter said, "He's my son. Call me Pete," and they asked what his son was called. "Most people call him Re-Pete on account of him always doing what I do."

THREE

Finding Hank's Journal

The Quarter-horse was a fine looking filly. It was healthy and recently checked over by the veterinarian. It came with all the proper paperwork to certify its status and value to the customer.

Peter and Hank were satisfied with the sale. They took some time to tend to their remaining horses. Young Hank used a rake and shovel to prepare each stable perfectly. When the rake's teeth became covered with clumps of horse manure he flipped it upside down to pull the clumps off onto the ground. With clean teeth the rake was good for digging into the hard dirt floor of the stable area. When it was clear of residual wastes, Hank was able to make nice grooves with the sharp prongs of the rake's teeth, all along the stable floor, without kicking up dust. The air felt clean when the floor was lighter than the weight of shit. He covered it with hay in the corners, near the trough of water that needed to be filtered with a fishing net and filled with clean water from the alley. The area was covered with a fresh dusting before any horse could enter.

Peter brought a pitchfork of hay before Hank, and the boy shouted in jubilation. I had never seen a child so excited over chores.

Peter said, "Hay for horses." His Italian accent was unmistakable, and it was rather endearing to hear him try to hide it anyway. Hank replied with an Italian Proverb, "*Battere il ferro finché è caldo*," which translates to: Make hay while the sun shines.

Before the sun was finished shining, the boy and his father had finished all their work at the stables. They left, and I followed them down the alley. I was almost positive they couldn't see me, but I still tried to remain in the shadows, along the line of fence and behind garbage cans, until they reached the cobblestones.

The cobblestone street was busy enough that I felt hidden in the crowds. I was at ease and found myself absorbed by the marketplace. The people were mostly merchants, closing their shops. There were a few townspeople trying to haggle over prices for fruit. One man was attempting to buy a book of Greek poems. He read one aloud, "She said, 'Most beautiful of things I leave is sunlight; after, is the glazing stars and the moon's face; then ripe cucumbers and apples and pears.' So wrote Praxilla." Taking in the world around me, I smelled delicious baked goods coming from someplace nearby.

Interestingly enough, Praxilla is the goddess we've chosen as the feminine face of all technology. It was this moment that brought her words to me at such a young age, and it seems fitting that her poetry stand as a shrine held by the strong arm of technology today. Our modern gods and goddesses speak to us all, outweighing the scripture they once wrote. They are granted immortality on our silvery screens, and they live forever in electronic fields that fill our skies. The inter-dimensional portals once were shielded, but when the greenhouse gas left civilization wrecked and crumbling, the heavens spilled over into our lands. 'The Hedges' was the subtle way I crafted to get people to turn back to looking upward.

I had lost sight of Peter and Re-Pete momentarily, so I followed the scent of pies. When I looked in through the glass of a shop ahead I saw them inside and saw the store was called Ma

Petite's Bakery. There, inside, was Ma herself. She greeted Pete and Hank.

Hank closed the shop door, locked it and started to count the register. The register drawer chimed, and all of a sudden I was transported back to my time as a teenager, helping hang drywall.

My grandfather was an old man again. I had missed out on seeing him grow older (just like Sherwood Lynch missed out on being there to see my mother grow older, I suppose). I missed seeing his hair turn grey when he was fifteen, when he saw Pete fall terribly ill. But I was able to read all about it when I noticed, there, along the asbestos drop-ceiling we were attempting to cover was a leather bound notebook, wrapped in hay bale rope. The book was a journal that Hank kept. He was trying to seal away those memories, but I found them before the drywall could be hung.

I felt that I deserved to know what happened and could learn from his memories. So I hid the book away. It was a selfish deed to do, instead of asking about what I found. I suppose, I didn't want anyone to take it from me before I could unlock its mystery. Looking back on it I bet my grandfather saw me hiding the book away, but he didn't say a word. He just kept painting. I joined him, and he said, "Looks like you might have found something you're good at."

He was wrong about what he said. I'm a terrible painter. I'm uneven with my brush-strokes. I use paint on wood, or canvass, without finesse. But I picked brightly colored words to paint pictures on the cave walls of the mind.

I wasn't a boxer, nor was I a painter. I was a poet. My heart told me to take Hank's journal and to write poetry, and that's what I did after he died.

. . .

You are not the only one
Who likes a little fun.
With tongue licks, woo,
And tummy round.
Jay Hedges chuckles too,
But Jay chuckles underground.
—*The Hedges*, issue no. 12

. . . .

FOUR

Joining the Circus

When I had the idea to pick up and move across the country, we left out of fear of judgment and thirst for exploration. I was the fear, and the one I was with was thirsty.

I enjoy the way Friedrich Schlegel described life on the fringe when he wrote, "The life of an artist should be distinguished from that of all other people, even in external habits. They are Brahmins, a higher cast, not ennobled by birth, however, but through deliberate self-initiation."

I chose to date a woman who my family did not approve of. I was met with hostility over dating a woman who was a different race than I. Our relationship was still new, and I had such fond memories from when I visited Chicago to pull us to the city. I had come on my own a few years prior for a few workshops on writing poetry. I had trained there before in an experiential art form with a literary foundation out of Saratoga Springs in Upper State New York, and the city, called the Windy City by many, had kept blowing its way to my heart.

When I visited the Windy City the first time, when I was alone, I met that man named Mark David Marks, who always wore paisley shirts with long sleeves to cover his enormous hands. He worked for the Make-A-Wish-For-Poetry Foundation, and he said he saw potential in me, so while I was visiting I decided to join him as a plant in the audience during his lectures on writing propaganda. I asked questions about a movie that was produced by one of the

25

sponsors of the event, *Cooler Runnings*. My impersonation of Hoffman in *Mrs. Robinson* was on point.

We thought it was worth trying out. To move us there, I maxed out several credit cards that I never could afford to pay back. To this day, when I get letters from debt collectors, asking for thousands of dollars and no delay, I try to focus on the words in bold print. Always to be found somewhere in their billowing explanations is the phrase YOU OWE NOTHING MORE. Of course there have to be more words along with that phrase to make sense of them sending the letter in the first place. But I've come to find out that by focusing on that phrase before and after opening their letters, and you must focus on that phrase exclusively with no reading of the rest of the letter, I promise the debt will appear to be no more, because it'll seem like you've read it from them that you owe nothing more.

I used the money to rent a moving truck and pay the first month of rent for my girlfriend at the time, and our two cats. That financial turmoil wouldn't let up. I thought I owed every last dime before I learned the trick mentioned above, so I tried to pay them back without delay. I worked as a baker when I wasn't slinging loglines and selling poems. Playwriting and acting became more than hobbies when I realized they could help pay for expenses.

In addition to feeling the pressure of a false economy, before the Great World Economic Reformation occurred, I felt I was entirely alone. She worked a few events as a spokesperson, and she even convinced her employers to use my poetry to market their products. This is where 'The Hedges' first started appearing as digital announcements on electronic devices held by people around the world. I first thought of that hedgehog character when I chose to write a piece for her family's farm, Forgotten Farms, which was changing its shape, using machines to pick crops instead of people. But I think back now, and I see her there sleeping most of the time. I felt like Schrödinger with his cats, but I was worse off, for I had a girlfriend that might have well not existed inside our one-bedroom apartment.

. . .

"Good afternoon," says Jay Hedges,
our notorious hedgehog friend,

"A fine day to witness dredges.
Such a day I wish never to end."

With all the wine,
With all the grape,
Jay scurries much
Making escape.
　　　　　　—The Hedges, issue no. 27

. . .

Love wasn't paying the bills, so they shut off the power, but I ran a cord for the refrigerator to the hallway outside of our unit. The landlord's lackadaisical legal maneuvers kept my experiment afloat. By the time we were officially evicted I had the idea to look for an alternative means of shelter. That was around the same time I auditioned for my first feature film since the program I worked on in elementary school. That was an educational series about technology, and bullying in schools.

I talked the seller of a mobile home down from three-thousand dollars to one-thousand. The money came in all at once when I decided upon the idea, and my girlfriend was relieved to hear the seller agree when I said, "I've got one-thousand dollars. Cash-in-hand."

We left to join the modern day circus, believing a lie about Vaudeville's resurgence. The cameras pointed, flashing bulbs blinked, and microphones earned sounds, all was quiet on set like nobody was around. The woman I was with fell in love with fashion. She tricked me into following my dream to write for the screen.

The movie I auditioned for wanted me to play the role of a drug-addled youth, but I declined participating in drug humor, stealing the line from Andy Kaufman, I paraphrased, "I don't find drug humor appealing. I won't be reading for that scene." They had me read for the part, which I read plainly without any emphasis whatsoever. But I blew them away when I read for the supporting role of James. I remember picturing the old farm truck sitting outside the space was mine, as I read words written for James to speak. That move earned me a supporting role, large enough for the woman designing the movie posters to ask how I spelled my last name. I told her my role wasn't large enough to have me featured on the posters. Humility goes far, and enough kindness won screen time with horror legends and reputable gore movie actors. Shaking hands with larger than life individuals might win the farm for most people, but I rather enjoyed the commitment of playing the role of James, a farmhand who was head over heels in love. The character was in love with one of the film's protagonists, played by a British woman who introduced us to all kinds of people off the set, most importantly, the freaks at Venice Beach; some of those freaks helped me get my poetry to the right people. She vanished like a real apparition while working on a horror film of her own.

"Cut, take a step back and think less about the lines that are on the page," said the director.

My core being identified with the writer I met at the audition, when I swore to uphold the words he wrote by taking a sacred part in this remote Hollywood Production, but I broke eventually. I said the lines how I thought the character would say them.

"That's better than what the scripts say. Do you write?"

They hired me to go over the script and make it better. I wouldn't be given credit, but the opportunity to see and hear my words come through on screen was enough for me.

We had been living in the mobile home in the little mining town outside of Chicago for over a month before production started. It was an easy town to get along with, as people accustomed to living on the fringe of society, for we were so well accustomed to this ourselves. I only remember getting hassled by the cops once for wearing my clown nose and tap dancing in the city square park of Galena. The rest of the time the cops left us alone because we were kind people, who introduced ourselves everywhere we went. This was how I was raised to be, and the girlfriend, who still spoke for the farm, was yet to turn into a regular high-end fashion model. We also had a good reason to be in their city. We were part of the motion picture business.

The girlfriend spoke on behalf of the farmers, and I helped spread those messages with 'The Hedges'. I didn't think twice about how 'The Hedges' were being used as propaganda.

People outside of the industry seldomly travel to Galena, but it's where stars like Ford and famous retired musicians go to play as a Mark Twain reenactor when they reach their golden years.

While it may be true and worth knowing that some of the more exclusive people in the motion picture business visit Galena, I make no assertion that we were exclusive at all. Still, people had plenty of questions for us because of the way we rode into their town. All I had to say is that I was getting ready for a role in a film, and the townsfolk, much like the cops, let us be. I had to promise to stop scaring tourists as well. I stopped tap dancing, and we met a seemingly benevolent woman who offered us a safe place to stay with our mobile home.

"Rolling. Sound speed. Okay, go ahead."

"Action."

I told her I loved her as the character would have. We had been in classes together and finally on a movie set, and it was what the character felt, yet it was only what *that* character felt.

"Good. Cut."

Meeting crews. Shaking hands. Big star comes up as I tie my shoe, before my character is shot in a scene we were filming that day. "Check that gun. Never make that mistake," says another Hollywood elite. He sits for an interview, and I agree to base the Jay Hedges character off of him, and off of Hank, I tell him.

"I'll stand up to say hello," I say.

"Something hasn't happened on this set. We haven't been introduced yet. I'm Sig."

We were filming the picture when I heard bad news from back home. I remember when we bought the mobile home I had to fix it up some. I patched the roof and stopped it from leaking. I was proud of the work I'd done on it, and I bragged to the woman I was dating, and I said to her that my grandfather would be proud of what I had learned, but he wasn't there to see what I had done on my own. I was keeping my family unit dry. It was a mobile unit, but I wouldn't let them get soaked in the rain. Sure not.

It stayed pretty dry the whole time. I never used the stove much, but I would use the electric burner I brought to make simple meals in a public park near pavilions that had outlets. I remember making too much oatmeal and pasta one night. I tried to consume all of it to avoid being wasteful, and threw up, right there in the park.

I hadn't been writing much poetry then. The only writing I was doing was for 'The Hedges' and scenes for the movie we were filming. But I did keep journals, and kept them impressively detailed. I made a few remarks that would later culminate into essays. I wrote so much prose that I ran out of paper, and I had to start making notebooks by hand, using my knowledge of bookbinding. I had a strange experience when I made one book. I made one notebook by hand, binding its pages with a twine I found at the farm we were parked at overnight, and strangely enough the words filled in themselves.

The first entry in the notebook was written by a seemingly loving mother and father, which seemed unlikely given that my parents divorced shortly after my birth. I doubted they would get together to write a message for me, but it said, "Stay strong! No matter how hard something may be! —Mom and Dad" I flipped through to find, to my surprise, the rest of the words were all written by Hank. They were signed at the bottom of each entry. The last entry in the journal was the date at which was present, and it contained a strong warning that I might never see the man who wrote the entries again. It read, "Your future is bright and bold, but my story has already been told."

31

I tried to show my companion but her glasses were too dark for her to see out of, and she just nodded. So I called Hank, for then I still had a phone. I lied and told my grandfather that I was training to be a boxer. I can remember him shouting with glee to my mother, who was nearby when I called him: "He's going to be a boxer!"

It seemed to me like he had believed it, but my mother can always tell when I lie. I didn't want to lie to him, but I knew he'd think a boxer was an admirable profession, so I figured there wasn't any harm in telling the lie.

My grandfather died before filming was finished. That's what the speaker told me on the electronic device. I grew distant, and nobody on the set would believe that someone I cared for had perished. Taking the leap from his coil, as the bard said. I took it well, I suppose. I have an understanding of death, which includes all the mourning procedures I've been taught. Hank's soul jumped from our tank. I tried to use it on set for inspiration, but my part was almost finished filming.

"Cut. Let's try something new. Keep it fresh," says the director.

Big shot actor in my scene loves the way I goof around in front of the camera: "You remind me of the guy who played Norman Bates in *Psycho*. You know who I mean?"

I brought my love an ice cream after tripping over a mop bucket. Her smile nearly melts the bowl, but I've seen that smile too often. She had a sex scene with an actor. "I once dated a woman who had a crush on you," I told the actor. I wasn't there when the scene was filmed; it was a closed set, I was told. I wasn't sure if I could ever think of her as mine again, which was something I soon realized.

After we wrapped, I brought the star to his house when I borrowed an assistant's car.

"Come inside," said Robby. "They finished the attic above my place. Smells like cedar." It smelled strong. I carried his bags because he was on his last leg, I could tell, and I thought about Hank who had just passed. Robby asked me if I wanted to go get a hotdog and hang out. I had stuck around a little while to chat with my friend, but I declined the hotdog. "Some other time," I said.

"Come back anytime you like," he said.

There wasn't any reason to practice reading our lines because the script was awful. My rewrites of the script were story driven, and the characters were interesting, so the producers hired the best paid performers they could afford, and a respectable director made the best out of my script.

Still, when I talked to the man from the foundation, the one that sought to reform poetry for use as propaganda in film, I told him it was going to be fine. Even though a producer had stolen many costumes before she quit, after her assistant accidentally burned down a barn we were using for the set of our film. I lied and said it was all going as planned.

"Are you achieving your dreams?" asked the man in paisley patterns.

"It's a dream alright. Every line they read is like a sonnet I wish I had wrote."

"But you are the writer after all."

FIVE

The End of a Legacy

I t makes sense that I'd be with a really pretty woman. I was always imagining it. What a narcissist I've been. It wasn't enough to date a model spokeswoman in the farming industry. Years later I found a woman who actually deserves to be a model, based on her works of service, wit, and her beauty. Natural beauty supercedes anything makeup and hot irons can do. But there was a time, I suppose, I could have married a fashion model. Too bad I found out she was a robot.

I had trouble starting off with the fashion model. Not because she was high class. I liked that about her and I still do. She rubbed off on me that way, like people always *do* influence each other. I remember when we fled our hometown because I feared being persecuted for my beliefs. I was in disbelief, and I still am. Two people coming together from different racial or ethnic backgrounds is beautiful to me. It was love and we both knew it, so I tried to give us a real chance by moving with her to a new city. When we moved into our apartment on North Ashland in Andersonville, we lived next to a strange neighborly and polite man with one eye and a heart of gold for charity work. But I recall how repulsed I was by goodwill, and how I heard him comment when I walked by with the fashion model on my arm. The neighbor had been talking with our landlord, long before he made our eviction, and I heard him reporting his observations about life, in general. Coincidentally, some words and phrases just so happened to come to his mind when we appeared in front of his unit. The landlord was pulling information from him as we moved down the hall towards our unit.

I heard the neighbor say, "Some women act like their shit don't stink."

Maybe that wasn't a race thing, and maybe none of it was. The thought occurred to me then: perhaps, I had a habit of taking one comment and letting my mind run with a single idea. It would run across the country and open up galleries, publish plays, even thought it could write for the screen. I started to have a vague realization in that moment in the hall on North Ashland Avenue: maybe the commentary was due to the way in which she was a highfalutin type, and everyone could tell it by the way she talked. Racial bias is undeniable, and I'm certain it existed. We didn't make everything up in our minds, did we?

She held her food in her hand, I remember, keeping the plate away from the table as we ate with my grandmother. Grandmother told her she didn't have to do that. But I also know I was doing it too because it seemed more poised and proper at that time. My grandmother didn't really care, so she didn't make a big to-do about the way we ate, or about race. Nevertheless, people came to tell me how I was killing her with my dating a woman of a different skin color. I don't think that was true at all, and I don't believe my grandmother would say it was true either. But not believing in stupid ideas doesn't stop other people from having them for themselves. So when she got sick, we packed up and left town.

There was a time where a friend told me that someone in my close nuclear family made an off-handed remark about "shooting the *chica* if he brings her to my house." Then, the fashion model's car was graffitied with symbols of hate. So we took off to see if we had what it took to make it. And we almost made it together all right, so I can't say I regret going off with her. Not in the least. I don't have feelings of romantic love for the model left over, however. I spent all those feelings driving back and forth across the country from Woodlawn to Beverly Hills. And back again, towards the tail end of our time together. I don't love her like that. Not any longer. But sometimes I love her as a friend does, and I miss having her around, as a friend does.

I returned home from where we fled. I came back to Woodlawn during that film production where I was playing a small town romantic named James. I left when I heard the news from my mother that my grandfather was on borrowed time, and that I should pay my last respects while he still had time. Now I find that my profession allows for that sort of payment to be dispersed throughout a long stretch of my poetic, rambling career, instead of paying all my respects in one lump sum. For, I may honor those ill, or deceased people with my famous poetry.

Oh! How that producer worried about me leaving set to never return again. I left on a puddle jumper of a plane from the old mining town, back to Woodlawn. I had a few days back home to see my family. I was there to see them, but I got mixed up with some old friends. Travis brought me to a bar downtown and Cassie met up with us to smoke some legal substance, a strange thing you could buy at gas stations in Maryland. It was called Possession.

When I got to my family's home, before I unleashed a rampage, ripping down smoke detectors, tearing thermostats off walls, and clawing at the wallpaper in Woodlawn Manor, I made time to have one last smoke with my grandfather out back. It was after he first saw me coming inside the house, after arriving at the farmhouse called Woodlawn Manor.

I came in like a demon, stumbling and looking for the worst kinds of fun. He told me I was up to no good. "You're coming in late like you were when you lived here, like you're out there doing things you shouldn't be doing." I took my aviator sunglasses off, since it was dark in the house. Laughing at his comment and the fact that it was nighttime, I folded the glasses, and then I folded them an extra time, creating a permanent crease along the nosepiece.

We smoked a cigarette out on the swing out back. My grandfather was weak, weaker than I had ever seen him before, and he talked like he was out of his mind. He was always sharp and full of wit, but suddenly he was warped. The drugs the doctors put him on to fight cancer and relieve pain had warped his perception. He told me something, and because of Possession I had considered it.

He talked about dying more than most people. Whenever he ran into a problem he couldn't fix, or if he felt that life was meaningless. This lesser quality that affects many people came out that night when he told me he was ready to die. I had heard him say things growing up, things like, "Gee, I wish this house would just burn down," so I guess when I heard him say, "Just fucking kill me already," I guess I wanted to call his bluff.

So I took him in to talk to my grandmother. We woke Fifi up. I wanted to talk to her about death, but the old timer pushed me a little, so I pushed him back. That was the one time in my life when I had any physical altercations with a member of my family. It was a gentle shoving match between a burn-out poet and an old man on his deathbed.

It scared my grandmother to see. Rightfully so. She called everyone in our family. They came over and held me down in bed until Possession had passed our house.

My grandfather forgave me for pushing him. It seemed to enliven him a little in a way. "You think you're strong. You think you're a boxer, but I could kick your ass," he said to me the next day. I came to make up for everything by planting some bushes in their front yard, and I started to touch up the blue paint on the porch because the color blue is said to ward off evil spirits since they can't cross over water. I suppose sometimes we need to be pushed a little.

He also told me then that he was accepting of me dating the fashion model, and he said, "I wouldn't mind seeing you both come through our front door telling me you got married."

I never married her though because when I was on that substance, I looked at the device to talk to her, and Possession helped me see clearly that I was dating a robot. I became sure of it. There was no convincing me otherwise.

SIX

Burning the Book

In the middle of the night I heard a voice call forth and wake me. It said:

"I could see you when I'm not around. When I go to sleep I go to a place where I can see. I can choose who I see when I go away. When I go away I go to that place. I fill the narrow space between the boards and beams with my breath. All the little critters are just people. Bugs and snakes, spiders and trapped flies, all of the critters I don't know treat me like the people I don't know. It doesn't worry me that people I don't know routinely turn from me. It used to piss me off but piss on them. They're sweaty and salted by the dusty places they've been. Their homes and the factories. Poor bastards, but what do I know? I left the bottle when it was my time. Do not become like me. Are you finished writing yet?"

Before leaving to confront my mother's father, the man I fear I'll become, I awoke from this vision that haunted me. I read the words on The Virgin of the Immaculate Conception to comfort me. I read aloud: "Non prote sedpro omnibvs hac lex constitvtaest." Words painted on a red book by Bartolomé Estaban Murilla.

Whenever I needed a reminder of who I was I'd ask myself who raised me and where I've lived since my upbringing, and I'm reminded of how being alive in the universe means more than following the teachings of our ancestors, and more than schools or streets can teach. How delicately I have unhinged from my strict puritan ways and my protestant upbringing. The Latin phrase meaning, "This law does not apply to you but all others," hovers on

39

top a painting that reminds me of how I was once nearly convinced by my mother to believe in the conception by immaculate means. Mother resented most men, seeing men as grotesque sexual beings, so she arranged for my puritan upbringing in hopes that I wouldn't become focused on the sensuality that befalls many, as it befell many of my ancestors. Generations of lost fathers that left to look for women elsewhere haunted mother's decisions of where to send her only child. In that way, the books of the cloth taught me to fear men, but I would eventually stop. That fear was cut off when throughout my childhood my father and his brother taught me courage by pulling me from rivers of torment.

I can trace back my father's genealogy as far as my mother's side, even with my mother being an adopted woman. Her father left her when she was small and still learning about life, so no wonder why she wanted me to believe in the immaculate conception. She probably even thought of herself as the Blessed Virgin.

Either way I'm thoroughly convinced now that, perhaps, behaviors, manners, occupations— even personalities— are things learned or adopted from our surroundings. For instance, my father's father held a steady job as a proficient typist, so my understanding of such inheritance is that I was, at any early age, more likely to develop an interest in typography. And I did inherit such interests, I believe. Though the poetic nature I aim to cultivate is moreso something the women whom I've been around have gifted to me through their kindness, and I kindly accept the responsibility to proceed eloquently on behalf of them, if I may.

However, to be so bold and write for the enjoyment of others seems to be a passing memento, unless it yields the same sting that death might harrow. To bring it up, as a hero might confront one's fears, I must.

I must, however, not forget to confront my empty void of inhumanity. I must taste the loss because victory has become too sweet, for my budding business unrolls its earthly roots, and my poetry pulls with vines attached to the tallest trees, and such word-play devours the dead skeletons of fallen ones. By using thick, crisp parchments that hang in the mid-air, as banners do, I project my thoughts to you. For, I know not what I am, but that I am a man for your dissection.

And now, as I approach the man who ought to have raised my mother, I fear that I will become him. Sherwood Lynch, the shadowy figure who might as well be dead to the world, for he has been dead to everyone I know and love. Let him witness my cold attitude. I come to his home without scorn for him, or for his chosen family, swinging upon this creaking porch chair, hung by rusted chains, but what's worse than the sound of the swing is the old hag's voice. She insults my patience by offering me coffee for a second time, but I say I am not thirsty. She gives me a shoebox filled with letters.

"He wanted to write you," she tells me, "to introduce himself to his kin, I suppose."

"But you wouldn't let him write me, huh?" I say with a satisfied shrug.

"He didn't find the right words," she says. "Each time he'd put his pen down, and he'd say he'd get back to it later. But he never sent them. I wouldn't have tried to stand in his way."

"I probably couldn't read his scratch," say I, before

unfolding one, and I only see the first few lines, the handwriting and care he was taking to know the truth, but I cannot relent from the fear. For, I am aware that a boy takes after his mother's father. Sherwood Lynch is what I could become!

This sickens me. The shadows of lust and lies consume my pure hearted nature. My quick wit wanes some. My palms tremble in knowing the truth. I am not a bastard, but if I was I'd be no worse off! If my mother was a whore, or my life cut short before I was even born. Such hell I might muck around in, but I would be no worse off. I leave the hag and his letters. I look in the mirror above the dashboard, and fear the battle I will have with time.

Memento mori confronts me when I open the leather bound book of Hank's. I read the journal I had found, the same words that filled the journal I once created, I find them again. Looking beyond the poetry hedged around those words, I find the guts inside of it are intensely interesting: notes about bloodshed in the Last Global War, and about the love of family. I even had the man who wrote the original book arrange photographs to fit with his passages before he died. Even so, when I read it now, and again, the book is not the same book to read. For, to read it, I am confronted by a new darkness.

The reminder of death spills from the pages of a journal that should give me such great joy to read. I pour through its pages with a candle to light the cab of my truck, and in the smoke I see him.

He's as grey as he always was. Though he's not as slim as he was when I last saw him. He's not sick; he's meaty and choking on a cloud of smoke. The smoke comes from every pore and surrounds him. It's not as ghastly as it sounds because he doesn't mind the smoke at all. He doesn't realize he's dead either. He sits in a recliner when he wants to relax. By the window he wonders why he doesn't bleed, nor get hurt the way he used to. He still fixes the house all the time, and drives for long periods of time, too. But he never leaks blood the way he used to when he was alive.

Like most people, I suppose, I picture death as the deterioration of life, but its form requires more careful attention. Considering my connection with life, such a book about its absence loses my interest. I start to draw smoke trails all over its pages. Tracing them, the reminder of death, *memento mori*, fades away when I capture the smoke on its pages. It speaks to me. I have no choice but to listen to it. I have no choice. It drowns my other senses. I try to put out the fire to get rid of the smoke.

The pages speak to me. They say, "I am what you will be." I confront the reminder of death, because I must stare it down, or it will take me over. I confront death by burning the journal over a fire. The fire of the candle I lit springs forth. My notebooks and packages of pencils burn up. The wicker shelf in my cab catches on fire easily. My towers of poems burn up like matches blazing in the night. All the propane I keep in the bed behind my mobile reading nook heats up.

The voice has become ashes that need no smoke to say, "I was what you are."

In a rage I can't stand, I take the ashes and squash them out in my hand with the hot red coals that burn and blister my fingers and hands.

After all the traveling and all the lecture hall symposiums, am I stubborn enough to burn up in my own vehicle? I extinguish it.

The fire sizzles beneath a few gallons of water, and the ceiling is only charred some, truly. That sizzle is the last I hear of the voice. It says, "For every man this is so."

The man I tried to emulate is gone. I realize who I am. I am going mad. For, in the middle of the night I packed my bags and swore off every person I knew. I loaded up my pickup that I was gifted by my mother's adopted father years ago. I parted ways with the Eastern Seaboard in search of a man. Not any man but the man I would soon become.

SEVEN

Permanent Parking at Sherwood's Lot

Galena, IL. April 15, 20—

My muse loves when I show up broken and stumbling.
Shortness of breath, my own, lends to every word I write. It's
as pure and easy to me as the breeze that draws near hair to
stick to brow, she sighs in relief because I brought the broken
soul of my own to her instead of living happy and dumb:

I'm damned by all for harvesting
what none want to take from.
Our core, and the lady of
words gifts the righteous ones
for me.
And I pass them to you.
H e r e —

—*Shane Sullivan*

"Well you're not going to have anywhere to go tonight, Shane," says the postman after we tried to move the tree, but it wouldn't budge from the truck.

I guffawed and said I'd walk to town. "When daylight comes back I'll purchase a chainsaw to remove the son-of-a-bitch."

His lips were flapping grotesquely with racial slurs about his neighbors who might've been African, but there's no way of telling, for he likely fantasized that I would feel some shallow form of

45

nepotism for him after he blamed them for growing the tree that fell on my truck, but I couldn't fall for the *geasa* this marauder offered. No. I looked closer to see that this very tree had been tampered with, perhaps earlier in the day, for just below the tree that fell is a deep gash in the bark that has green around its edges.

"I hate a tree to grow so close to my house. Sorry you had to get the brunt of its fall, but perhaps you'll stay until we get your truck unstuck."

The postman brought out an axe, but I wouldn't accept help, nor would I swing at my old Ranger. He put the axe away and went to make dinner, while I studied the way the tree laid on the hood and pinned my truck down flat to the ground. The glass from the passenger window kept crackling and chattering in conversation with itself. Nature had brought me into the world, and it has caused my mother's father to run off and leave my mother to grow up without a dad, but nature hadn't had enough apparently.

Gravity thinks it will keep the lock closed on my stay this night. Surely that old scoundrel didn't feel right telling me to get on down the road with my transportation paused on his lot. He had assured me that it was an act of God, but I could tell right away he had taken a chunk away from the tree before I got there.

When he saw how I examined the bark of the fallen tree, where it had been removed through force and left to fall on its own, onto my truck—that's when he spoke up. "You can sit for dinner and stay tonight if you'd like."

I stressed how it appeared that I had no choice in the matter, and I doubt that he missed sensing how I was near weeping by the stinging look about my eyes. I sat next to the scene, and now I write about what I had been putting off writing all day. I drove to see that scoundrel, and left behind everyone who cared for me. And now I've lost the only thing that had worked right. I lost everything when that tree fell. I've given up so much, but now my situation is ruined.

It all started when I didn't feel like writing anymore articles for Miss Kirkpatrick. I wanted to help save the farms, instead of helping the big chemical companies push poison on us all. "There's no better place to grow," I think, and I write:

> *Growing from the soil,*
> *the hedgehog's life is*
> *full of dirt—*

But mine, unlike the Bard's mortal coil, cannot get the right word out about the tiny character I've crafted. Jay Hedges, my hedgehog cartoon, my most notorious character. He drinks all the wine, eats strawberries without permission, and helps everyone get over the machines being the new farmers.

But out from the dust where the tree is firmly rooted sprouts a plant worthy of measurement, but no carpenter could produce tape firm enough nor rule long enough to chart it before it grows twice the height of the old tree. "I see you're writing about the forgotten farm," says a voice that stops me before I can finish with the first stanza of my poem. I don't feel worthy of talking to a tree tonight, and I don't think there is any use in trying to get the old postman to cooperate in corroborating the strange occurrence, so I go back to writing.

"The forgotten farm could use a visit," says the persistent voice.

"I don't know who you are, or where you are," I say finally.

47

"Come around," says the voice, so I move around the base of the newly grown trunk. I am half-expecting to see a local nitwit playing tricks on me. Yet, there in the bark of the tree protrudes a speaking mouth and eyes creeping in from both sides.

"You're going to need to take a ride out of here before sunrise if you're going to make any change," says the face in the tree.

"Change?" I ask. "What do you know? You're just a face on a tree that sprouted up today."

"I am in tune with nature better than you can imagine," says the face. "I know your poetry is going to influence the stakeholders at Forgotten Farms, and you aren't going to write it the right way, unless you leave here before sunrise tomorrow."

The problem with my truck being crushed no longer seems so large to me. In this moment, looking at the face of a man ingrained in the wood—I suppose it's a man's face, because it sounds like a man, but there isn't much of a mustache or jaw like a man usually has. Well, I suppose the magically growing tree might be right about getting on down the road, so I leave my truck there where it sits.

On my way out, I smell the air. The old postman is cooking breakfast for dinner, I suppose. I bail on confronting him again. He can keep my truck.

EIGHT

On the Road Out of Tennessee

On the road, I am unsure of which way to go since I abandoned my vehicle containing maps of the area. I'm unfamiliar with the area, but I know I have to keep on the move because it is my destiny to use words to help others.

. . .

> *Spikey, and plump round skin*
> *Machines won't get the best of him.*
> *If he's fit, be he fast,*
> *And if he's full, days he'll last.*
> *Jay Hedges lives alone,*
> > *below fields of crop.*
> *His hunger, his dream of sweetness,*
> > *will never stop.*
> —The Hedges, issue no. 35

. . .

The tree that fell from Lynch's property might have crushed my truck but I feel full of purpose still. I find a neighbor in the Tennessee town of Chattahoochee is giving away a bicycle, but when I arrive I find out that all the decent bikes are too small for me to ride. I've been giving some thought for some time now about converting to a cycling lifestyle; after all, Hemmingway used to marvel over cycling, so it must be fit for something, I suppose.

The bicycle I ride off on is in desperate need of repair. I find a gas station and air up the tires. I find the back tire holds air nicely, which is perhaps the only working aspect of the bicycle, apart from the rusty chain and tight handlebars. Perhaps the worst part about the bike is the lack of pedals. The previous owner scrapped parts from the simple machine. Instead of pedals, there are holes in the cranks where pedals should live.

I put a thick bolt through a hole in one of the cranks. I only find one bolt while searching the gas station lot. I refuse to go back to the postman for assistance in the matter, for talking to him was like looking into a mirror filled with disappointment looking back at me. I try to leave the image behind, and I pedal.

I'm able to rotate the sprockets of the single speed bicycle by using the one pedal that I've crafted out of the bolt, but it's slow going with one pedal. I have to move the bolt all the way around by using the top of my foot to complete each rotation. It's tiring, and requires a lot of effort.

On the way up the hill, the only living creature I encounter is a fly as I am pedaling. As I am pedaling up the hill, I swallow him whole. And instantly I feel a pain in my stomach, an intense burning, partly because I'm nervous. I'm nervous for the fly. I try to cough it up, and regurgitate the simple creature because nothing should have to experience such a swift, disturbing mortality. But my stomach doesn't give up the winged thing. As I cough and try to empty my insides of everything I hold, I come to a vague realization that there's nothing to be done for it. As my stoic friends have said, fate would condition our futures, and, "The fate of a fly is the fate of the spider."

I still relinquish much regard for the creature: with such a short life already, how unfortunate it is to have its candle of life put out so soon; it surely saw me as a large monster with a slick, fleshy throat. I sucked that fly up like I was cleaning the air of debris, and as the acids within my body ate away its wings—"Bb-zz-t"—it could fly no more, and only blames my intrusion, of course. Surely I am to blame.

But I'm moving along at a decent speed when I see ahead of me, on the side of the road, signs for a road closure. Apparently, a bridge is out up ahead, but I'm not too concerned because I've encountered road closures while driving my truck in the past, and after making way up this steep hill I consider myself a seasoned cyclist already. By now I have already imagined carrying my bicycle across many streams, and I've imagined braving the mightiest rivers on the planet as well. I've sat in Elizabeth, Illinois, near the Mighty Mississippi, and I'm sure I could make it, crossing it with a bike over my shoulders. I'll take my chances on this little Chattahoochee River. When I reach the end of the road I notice the pedal I've fashioned is nearly about to fall off, so I tighten the nut on my homemade bike part before attempting to cross the river.

The bank of the river is shallow enough to make it into the freezing waters without much trouble. I start crossing the river, moving my feet in small steps out of an uncertainty of what lies beneath the rushing water. The Chorus from *Agamemnon* sings in my head, and Aeschylus wrote for me a chant, I say, "Sing sorrow, sorrow: but good wins out in the end."

When I am nearly to the other side of the river I find the water is higher than before, higher than I first expected it to be. It's nearly up to my neck! I thought I had imagined the worst of this sort of thing when I imagined what it would be like to cross the Mississippi, but I struggle to keep the bicycle raised above my head, singing, "Sing sorrow, sorrow: but the good win out in the end."

All at once I lose my footing and the bicycle is no longer in my grasp. I must have slipped on some algae on a rock at the bottom of the river. The water removes my bike from me, and I never see the piece of junk emerge.

Suddenly, leaving before sunrise, and taking the advice of a face speaking to me from the bark of a tree, seems like a poor idea. But I wasn't feeling so welcomed where I once was, and since I didn't feel welcomed there, it seemed like a better idea at the time to leave at night. That's why I left at night and wandered out into the cold, dark, unfamiliar setting. I thought it was my destiny to get on the road and help the forgotten farm return to its prime. But come to think of it, I had looked at the map of the area while waiting around for Lynch after the old hag came out to meet me, and I don't remember there being any river nearby.

Fancy me floating downstream. It isn't a problem. Floating downstream isn't a problem at all. After the sight of death and the poisonous smoke I have inhaled, I feel no pain as I drift through the waters. But why? The icy surface would normally sting the senses of most people, I am aware. But it doesn't bother me at all. It's just another sensation I must live with as I continue to move downstream. "Sing sorrow, sorrow: but good will win out in the end."

Rocks along the rapids put a stop to my floating and offer some form of natural bridge to allow me to get out from the river at last. However, when I climb onto the shore I am greeted by curious, flying apparitions that seem alarmed by my presence. They request proof that I am who I say I am. I show them my identification and they leave me alone. It appears they feel sorrow as a primary emotion. Yet, of what I have called about with my chanting, I do not know, for these beings are woeful as their constant state of existence, and they question me about anything they can think to question me about before leaving me for good.

"Where're you coming from?"

"Woodlawn."

"Where are you going?"

"The forgotten farm."

"What is your purpose?"

"To save a family farm."

"Why do you think you can make a difference?"

"I've already dedicated my life to making a difference," I say to the apparitions.

"Why?"

"Because others have not."

"Yes. But how so?"

"How?"

"How will you make a difference?"

"Through poetries."

NINE

A Shocking Realization

good man died so that I might plunder around the world on a poetic license, spending my small inheritance to reach far off destinations, pinning my poetry to bulletin boards, and nailing poems to telephone poles. My words and rhymes fit to hang from the totem poles of our times. I've spent a small fortune planting my flag where those that came before me had planted their own flags. My fate feels determined but I'm willing to read between the lines, to figure out what drives humanity, and to find out what drives the human spirit.

Plato described to me the type of emotion that I aim to capture. In *The Pine Grove*, his epigram instructs: "Sit below the high needles of the noisy pine as its branches shudder in the western winds. A shepherd's piping by the loquacious river will lay mammoth sleep on your spellbound eyelids."

My pen sails across pages of the finest parchment, I can't remember purchasing. And I feel no pain. I've watched the dead sit in armchairs in smoke-filled rooms, and I've survived the rushing cold waters, right? It can't be much worse than that. It can't get much worse. I'll write a sonnet for the poetry foundation to publish. The verses will light up people's minds when millions of people open the newsletter to read the news the foundation sends. The foundation I speak of has such an outlet to reach millions through cybernetic, digitally complex means. The internet is my friend. Technology is my friend. I dated a robot once, but that was in the past. Now, I've got to get my message to the foundation. I've got to show the world what's important and what we should strive to save.

My true beloved waits for me to call, but she'll have to hold tight and wait. I am forgetting her face. My memories blend together like watercolor paints when they accidentally get wet. For a stark contrast, my sonnet requires our love, so I cannot forget about our love. For, the verses must impress all the sensuous impulses, which only love knows truest. But it's hard to find such a tumultuous vocabulary, and my palette it weakly covered in blotches of unconscious coloring because I'm still stuck writing ballads for the owner of Forgotten Farms, my ex-girlfriend, Ashley Forgettes. She helped me find a job on the farm briefly, before the mandate of robot workers, and before I learned that dedicating my life-force to poetry was absolutely a must. If I wanted to be taken seriously by readers, by the foundation, and by the world, I knew I needed to breath and bleed for it.

The words are coming out smoothly over the parchment, and I don't even need to pause to count syl-la-bles because I know they're right. They have to be right. They come out like my pulse does. They're within me like my blood vessels are, but they aren't just for me: poetry's the white blood cell that gives strength to other ideas. Greater ideas. This one is moving right along. I left at sunrise like the face in the tree instructed because it must have known. The face is part of the natural world, so it must have known better than I know, even though I'm part of nature because I'm alive, right?

The face in the tree must have worked with nature to concoct the strange *sircumstances* that brought me harrowing across the river. It must have known I'd slip, and I fell down just like nature planned.

But why am I not injured? Why haven't I gotten a scratch on my surface? I should be mangled, or at least bleeding from the way I slammed into that rock that stopped me from floating farther down the river, but I am fine. I called it luck, but what do I know? Could there be more at play other than the strange talking tree at Lynch's lot?

After much deliberation, I am close to accepting that fate has it written down somewhere that I should be alive, that I should write by the river today, and that I should save Forgotten Farms. Who else is better off to capture Ashley's radiance than I? Nobody has lived the life I've lived as a scholar raised in Randallstown, whose parents are from Woodlawn. If a child's father and mother are from a place, then the child may choose to call that place their home as well. Or else I'll be the lost poet from Randallstown or Gwynn Oak, but it doesn't have the same ring to it, does it?

Woodlawn may not be my birthplace, but I choose it for my namesake. I lived there for years growing up. I've biked through it before, and I've even been arrested there once. I've grown out of those ways since. Now, I only want to give back to the place by claiming it as my name, and why not? I lived a block away from the Knights of Columbus, where I would ride my mountain bike as a child, from my father's street down that giant hill on Windsor Mill Road.

Every drop of ink is a letter imprinted on time that I cannot return, and it moves like the river has rushed, with or without me in it. But wait! How did my parchment stay dry? I didn't have a chance to protect it when I slipped. It should have been washed away like the bicycle with its missing pedals.

I've thought about it too long. I've lost the parchment and everything I had written is crumbling before my eyes. It transforms with the wet drops of rain falling from the sky. I'm holding what feels like mushy cardboard, and it runs with red and blue inks. But wait. My pen is blue! So where did the red come from? It's not ink. It's got to be blood. I've got to be bleeding, but I'm not seeing any gash anywhere. As I search my body for wounds, I find a clear abrasion alright. My awareness was not as keen as I had thought, for I'm not as isolated as I once thought I was. In fact, the river is dry, except for the rain that bounces ontop what now appears to me to be asphalt. I'm at the top of the hill on Windsor Mill, near Somerset Drive, near my father's house, and I'm awakened by its beautiful nostalgia.

Everything around is fuzzy and my living eyes need to adjust to the light of the sun. Where was I? My legs move and warm muscles have materialized enough to carry me down the road toward the shops. I feel full of life, like I remember once feeling. But it's not another distant memory from childhood. I've been numb for too long.

The Knights of Columbus building is on the left side of the road, past a wooden sign with geese painted on it. The sign is chipped, but, strangely enough, I've always remembered the sign being a pristine landmark at the town square in Woodlawn. A sign of community and brotherly love. My mother is there. She's nearly to her car, and when she sees me there she drops a handful of lottery tickets she had just purchased from the Knights.

She's in shock and I don't know why.

"You look surprised to see me back in town already," I say to her with my head hanging shamefully low.

"Shane," she says, "I'm surprised to see you alive."

"What do you mean?" I ask her.

"I mean," she grabs me and hugs me, "there was a fire at your apartment, my son. My son! You've been dead to the world."

PART TWO:

"SOME THINGS CAN'T BE UNSEEN,"

ONE

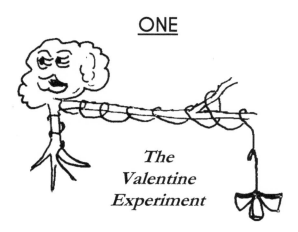

The Valentine Experiment

y vision cleared up when my mother bopped me on the top of my head and pushed me into her pickup truck. She took off with me, and my head was pounding bad enough for me to start sobbing.

"Here, take this," she said, handing me a half-empty water bottle. It was ice cold, and I noticed the paper label was shredded off the plastic bottle.

"We might have given you too much to drink this morning," she told me. I looked at her until she explained herself. "Coming back ain't easy. After the reconstruction, liquor is the only way we've been able to stop the conscious mind from panicking too, and going into shock."

We drove past a gas station that was shut down after what must have been a disaster to witness. The caution tape kept people from walking through the leftover debris, from what must have been an explosion at the gas pumps nearby. Black charcoal outlines of a car that had been removed still remained on the pavement near the pumps. A NO SMOKING sign, one ripped from the wall by the explosion, remained planted beneath the tape as well.

At a bus stop nearby, a man looked at his telephone for entertainment, but he focused on it like the information was a divine prophesy, like a soldier stays connected to his device during an air strike. He played with its light-screen. The light arranged on the screen to tell him how his bus was on its way, so he stepped out in the street for boarding.

"We'll have you checked over by Dr. Val—Don't worry. It's going to be—Oh!" mother shouted as I instinctively grabbed the steering wheel to swerve the pickup, and we missed hitting that man in the street. Instead, we hit a large granite rock that bent the bumper severely.

"That careless slob," mother exclaimed. "You can cuss, you know," she said.

"I know," I said and told her how I didn't feel like it.

"This world is falling apart, and we all know why," she said, and she rolled down her window to yell out at the man. "Take a look out before you cross next time!" That man waddled back to the bus stop, probably to relax for a little while longer before his bus came. Probably to let Praxilla's lovely tone take over his soul, and into her sweet surrender his consciousness crept when we left him there.

"How long was I . . . you know . . . . How long was I out for?" I asked. I was looking for answers to help clear up my headache.

"Not long," she said. "We used my memory to reconstruct living tissues. Dr. Valentine will help explain things better."

The neighborhood was nice, I remember from when I was young. Houses were newly built. They looked nice, but they were nothing when compared to the endless fields that were there long before. When I saw the houses in the doctor's neighborhood for the first time in several years, I remembered thinking to myself how I'd never want to live in a house that looks like everyone else's house, and now I remember talking with my grandfather about how anyone who purchases such a house must be a sucker with zero home-improvement skills. Now we're parked in the driveway of one of the houses in this cookie cutter neighborhood, and for some odd reason I couldn't be happier to be here.

I'm reeling for answers for what happened to me. I want to know what I should expect. Why do I feel immortal? I survived death and lived to tell what the afterlife is like, but am I lucky to be alive? For, what is in store for me awaits inside a plain home in this cul-de-sac that I remember wishing wasn't ever built in the first place.

My mother keeps quiet until she receives the signal to come inside. The porch light flickers once, and we unload from the pickup. She kicks at the bumper with her new, balanced sneakers, scuffing their pristine white sides. The bumper is bent alright, but there's nothing we can do about it now. She takes a crate of goods from the bed of the pickup, and she puts them on my arms before picking up a few jugs of water.

"Are we staying long?" I ask.

"You really don't get it, do you?" she asks me. "The dust storms and sudden fallout blasts are regular occurrences." She smiles politely before saying, "Get the door, sweetie."

I open the screen door to enter Valentine's home. The walls are lined with diagrams of machines that I don't recall seeing before. Plenty more blueprints are rolled up in the corner. Valentine is seated behind a manual typewriter on the upper level of the split foyer.

"We make an effort to not look at screens," she says. "People like that man we almost hit today are idiots who are letting our world go to waste. They suck up prophecy. We hardly need *The Hedges* to convince them nowadays."

We sit at a table near Valentine, who says, "Hullo and welcome back to the conscious resistance, la résistance, if you will, or what have you. We're decentralizing all technological intelligence to better live on this planet."

"Hi," I say.

He hits the keys in staccato for a few dozen lines of text to appear rather rapidly on plain vellum paper, while I try my hardest to wrap my warped mind around what has happened to me.

"Have I been dreaming?" I finally ask.

"Not so," says Valentine. "You've been seeing what's really there in the afterlife, sort of like this old machine. Nobody else knows what you saw but you." He types something I can't see.

"It's not that simple," I say. "I've had to witness some horrible things. In the great beyond, I've seen people who've died and . . . people I've never met before."

"We're learning more about life from learning about death. But not so the other way around. Death is still a mystery, but we're able to piece some of it together. I hope this helps. We're learning so much more, and more as we go," says Valentine. "From what I gather, being dead doesn't always feel like anything different than being alive. For your case especially because of the way in which you left with urgency. When you leave life without knowing you're on your way out from the building, it's hard to feel the change. I guess someone who knows they're dying, from a disease or cancer, for instance, would feel the progression towards death."

"Those people would have an easier time dealing with death if they are able to find peace before they go," says mother. "You never knew you left, since you only left a little while ago, so bringing you back was easier for your mind to deal with."

"Right. How much did I have to drink?" I ask.

They look at each other for a moment. "Not much," mother finally says.

"How were you able to bring me back?" I ask. I pick up a bottle of wine to smell its contents. "Did you just think of me and I appeared?"

"I wish it was that easy," says the doctor. "Do you think he's ready to go downstairs?" he asks mother.

"What's downstairs?" I have to ask.

The lower level of the split foyer is lined with fish tanks. The tanks are filled with coral and exotic fish, both of which ebb and flow fantastically when the doctor turns on the switch to power the neon fluorescent tubes covering the ceiling.

"The coral is alive," says the doctor who provokes it some. The bright green brain coral shrinks some when it's provoked. "It's a conscious entity that helps produce enough lower frequency brain waves, so many in fact that we are able to siphon some into this machine." From a small storage closet, Dr. Valentine wheels out a machine strapped to a tea cart. When he unveils it, then drops the cloth, mother plugs the strange mechanism into a wall outlet to cause its iridescent glow. It makes a loud whirring sound and lights up along its sharp edges.

"This is how we were able to bring you back to life, Shane," says mother. "You were the first one."

"Because you were burned up so recently," says Valentine, "made your mother's job easier. I found her and asked, and of course. What mother wouldn't want their son back?" The doctor smiles and nods a few times.

"You picked me because it was recent?" I ask.

"That's not all," Valentine says. "I need something in return, seeing as we've allowed you to return."

TWO

The Pain of Being Alive

The wine I drink came from a vineyard in Northern California, a place I recall visiting. At least I think I visited it. My memories are in disarray. I don't know what to believe. They assure me the feeling is one to pass. Perhaps I should begin again:

"You're going to be all right," says mother. This calms me some, and I actually begin to sit, and instinctively, I meditate with the uncorked vino holding me upward. Its cork nowhere to be found, the green glass bottle rests in the crook of my folded knee. My legs feel stiffer than I remember them being. My knees crack and pop, but I hold the pose and keep my eyes closed. My hamstrings are under more stress than they were while laying flat in a hospital bed and getting ready for a burial shroud. I can't even imagine the pain mother must have went through, so I let those thoughts melt away.

From his typing area, Sonny Valentine reads aloud, in a booming voice that reverberates in the basement where I sit.

"That sounds familiar," I say. "What is it you're reading?"

"*Frankenstein*," he says with a laugh, "by Mary Shelley."

Dr. Valentine places a pistol on the table next to one of the fish tanks where the flakes of fish food and cleaning supplies are neatly kept. The tanks are especially clear, so I ask about the fish because I can tell his expressions are those of pride. The way they're kept tidy, amidst the turmoil bubbling outside baffled me when I first came upon their aquatic luminescence. "I thought you'd ask about the gun," says Valentine, dodging a discussion about the aquariums.

"Guns don't bother me," I tell him. "You were probably expecting Frankenstein's Monster when she brought me here. I understand the need for protection."

He shakes his head and says, "I'm not afraid of you, kid. When we turned you loose we knew you were bright enough to find your way back when your mind cleared up some."

"I'm smart enough not to do anything stupid to get a quick dollar, hard-working enough not to starve, and creative enough to climb from the ashes yet again," I tell him. "But what if I was found out to be raised from the dead?"

He shakes his head again and says, "Angry village people with their pitchforks and torches. That's why I call this little beauty my fire extinguisher." He unloads the gun and reassures me again, "Not for you."

"I keep feeling like I'm remembering something, but it could all be my mind playing tricks on me," I tell him.

"It'll clear up," my mom says.

"We don't know that," I tell her.

"We don't," agrees the doctor.

"But it'll get better," mother assures me, "or you'll have to get used to it. That much we know is true."

"I guess that's something to look forward to," I say, trying to hold onto this moment as the only true thing I have got that is verifiably true, but, something that dawns on me pushes me to say, "How do I know I'm not dead now and this isn't a dream in the afterlife?"

"I figured we might have this conversation," says the doctor. "This neuro, biological nanu-circuitry is an experiment. At best it is a well-respected hobby. And I'm merely a hobbyist with drawings and blueprints from years of research. Some of my research is on you."

"I don't understand. What about my truck?" I ask.

"You've been riding a bicycle for years," she says. "A great big tree fell upon your truck and squashed it to smithereens."

"That's what I remember it being like in the afterlife," I tell them.

"It's possible that you were reconstructing memories to make sense of where you were," says Valentine.

"Well, that makes enough sense that I use a bicycle to get around," I admit. "You know, Hemmingway used to write about cyclists."

"He's a clever feller," says Valentine. "There's something else. Where's Lilloo? I wish she were here for this part."

"Lilloo?" And suddenly I realize the reason why Valentine seemed so familiar to me was that—not only was Valentine involved in my awakening from whatever hell I had imagined—the tormented visions I witnessed when visiting that vicious monster named Lynch—but he was also a participant in the background of my life at any early age. For, I was the focal point, the innocent, involuntary participant in one of his most well regarded yet ethically confounding experiments. The Valentine Experiment brought emotional intelligence and spiritual awareness to the automated kind.

"Yes," says Valentine, "much of this knowledge was to bring you back, however, most of it has been around since the ancients walked this planet. Do you see? I am not a doctor of the human body, or, of computer sciences, et cetera. I'm a doctor of the mind. And your mind has been my laboratory more than you could ever understand." Mother promises to tell me the truth about Valentine's experiments. All I really know is they were using artificial intelligence to test my emotional responses when I was a child. She promises to tell me everything.

"Your mother and I have discussed how this conversation might go," says Valentine, "and we've come up with a simple list. There's a way for you to cope with the frustration between reality and what your mind creates, but you'll have to remain calm. This is a bumpy ride, I'll admit."

"You made a list," I say, corking the vino. "What a way to pass the time."

"There are some definite characteristics of life that death cannot replicate, even in the vast expansion that makes up the eternal conscious mind."

"Pain is the first," says mother. My hamstrings pop out of place. The muscles are rejoicing over having fresh blood to circulate through my veins, but the pressure I give them in my seated lotus position is too much to bear. It's excruciating. I am in tears, but I remain focused on the sound of their voices, still happy to be alive.

"The human condition relinquishes its control when pain is experienced," says the doctor. "To force itself to feel pain, loss, or degradation is counter-intuitive. In death, we fear the burden of pain experienced in existence, so we are aroused to choose less seemingly painful pathways. But death is like a dream in this regard."

"You don't get hurt in dreams, right?" mother asks.

"Right," I quit biting my tongue long enough to admit.

"You can't get hurt in death either," she speculates, "because there's no more dying when you're buried underground."

71

"You brought me back to feel the horrors of existing," I say with a smile across my face.

"There you have it," says the doctor.

I laugh through the stretch and my rigor mortis truly vanishes overtime. "I feel like I've ran a marathon. My legs hurt something terrible."

"Well," says mother, "pain is part of life. Welcome back, sonny boy."

Pain of existence passes when I keep focused on my breath and the glorious feeling of life that no pain can defeat. Even the bloodiest battles, where wounded soldiers fought for their last breaths, are filled with the fight for life. When we, living hosts, outgrew our hostility, we put down the weapons and pitched in rebuilding the world.

After the climate fell apart keeping peace became easy to strive for, because our planet filled with chaos from natural backlashes. The grounds split, flooding became a regular occurrence, and lightning storms danced about the skies of mostly every continent. History was written as a time of temporary global peace while humans worked together.

There were uncouth groups of course, but nothing mattered from those groups. They would stage a coup to take over a facility or control a machine, but a few unorganized radical groups of kamikaze, technophobic, steamy raiders couldn't upset the balance of global peace.

It's that careful balance 'The Hedges' worked to facilitate by showing the cute cartoon hedgehog benefiting from machines, and machines made it so we don't have to work if we don't want to work. They feed us, and they save the planet. But sometimes the can be pesky, in my own opinion. The noise and bright lights. The afterlife had none of it. That afterlife was far simpler with less automobiles covering the streets and less machines dominating minds. My spirit blended with such natural elements, so much so that even the trees spoke to my kindred soul.

In a sense, machines fixing the planet makes nature happier, so the raiders are the real enemy, not the machines. And to stop the enemy would be preferred.

"You want me to write another hedge?" I ask.

"No," says mother.

"Valentine wants a hedge," I say. "I told you I'd write more."

"We have enough of those," says mother.

"Okay," I say. "Well, I can write something else. I've got another sleeve."

"You might have another trick," says Valentine. "You'll write for them again surely. But we need something else."

"What else do I know?" I humbly ask.

"You've experienced something that we can use to show the raiders, something about human & machine relations."

"Explain why we want anything to do with those pirate people," mother instructs. "Shane remembers how we lost many of our own."

"I see," says Valentine. "Your next role will be to show our enemy a way to right their own wrongs. I want you to think about what you'd say if you were Jay Hedges."

THREE

The Worst Types, and Their Solution

"It takes the worst types of people to survive the dust clouds. The acid rain pours through, and everything becomes measly. The people alive today must relent to the toxic way of their ancestor's habits. The atmosphere is like a dirty pool of water, like a swimming pool without filtration. Instead of allowing for our own destruction, we've created a way to shock the system. Together, we have saved the planet," says a talking fish in the tank in the basement of Dr. Valentine's home. I stay calm and focus on my breathing. I can hear the grainy sounds, of whirring motors, and vacuum pumps outside, in the skies above us, cleansing the area.

"They make it better," said Valentine. He tried to explain the new machinery to me: they clean the air and don't emit gasses. "They do what a filter feeder does for my tank," he said. Now, whenever I am troubled by the prevalence of technology I have this memory.

The fish in the tank thought they were wiser than humankind. "At least we clean up after ourselves," says a filter fish. And the clams cascade their vocations across chords, sounding of the ocean's wetness. That loopy lullaby alarmed me at first, as much as every babbling brook I can recall.

. . .

I can recall such a brook
that babbled kindly.

Some things I recall
drab, in my mind. Flee
to a soulful brook. I
recall its nature bubbly.

. . .

When I feel their turbines roar above me, I know it's for the better. Since I am made of glass, I remain still. Filled with stillness. They are the fish! We keep each other, for they are nothing without serving our needs.

"A god would be bored," says a lucky little crab who left his seaweed house, and he leaves the tank in the same stride, leaving drips as he goes.

"I'll stay still," I say to the crab, and I listen to the greatest salsa musician of the sea playing a ballad on an upright bass: upon a large set of stones at the bottom of the tank, Oscar spins the seashell he plays. He slaps its seaweed strings, and he dances with that thing. When he stops playing, his voice reminds me of Oscar D'Leon when the fish says, "It takes the worst types to survive this living death. You lived it, so you know. To survive it again? That's not easy. Without that doctor restarting whatever string connects your soul to your body, you wouldn't be here. You wouldn't be alive. Do you hear me?"

I reply with the words of a proud promulgator before me.

"What is that?" asks the fish. "Is that Percy Shelley?"

"Yes," I say. "That's from *Fragment on Reform*."

"I know," says the fish.

75

I find it impossible to communicate with fish. I swear, when I speak he must only hear air bubbles, but I try anyhow. I say, "Get out of my head. It's an illusion! I'm alive!"

When I yell I must wake someone upstairs inside the house, because I can hear footsteps coming down the stairs:

RA-THUMP-BA-THUMP,
RA-THUMP-BA-THUMP,
RA-THUMP-BA-THUMP!

I'm not alone in the room. I'm not alone. My mother is here. I can see her above me. She's picking me up, but I slide to the ground. My oily scales bend and twitch. My tail and fins have spines that might hurt her soft hands.

"I'm sorry, Ma!" I shout. I'm the fish from the tank that I've been watching all along. I left my family. I left everyone I ever loved to follow a dream. When the dream died, I was still alive, "AND I'M STILL ALIVE NOW!" I shout.

She shakes me away from the illusions, away from the visions. "This kind of stuff is natural," says Dr. Valentine, "when someone is to be reconstructed. Trust the process, Shane. You seem better off alive."

"Yes," I say, but I am still tormented. "They make it sound like I'm the machine."

"Don't be silly," says the doctor. My mother promises to tell me the truth about the observations during my childhood. We put the shade up again and raise the window shields to let some light in. Soon after the machines have finished hovering all is calm. They cleaned the air. They cleared the atmosphere above the house.

"I'm not usually this quiet," I admit, as I study the drawings and imagine the machines for myself. The schematics and blueprints hanging on the walls give me a good idea of what is flying above the area. I imagine the mechanical monsters.

"It makes sense that you've been seeing these things," mother says to me. "You've been sitting too close to the tank."

The doctor's recent creation of a fish resembling Frankenstein's Monster recites text from the source volume which Valentine had been programming. Franken-Fish looked lonely, so I release a fish modeled after Mary's husband, Percy. The politically charged Romantic-Fish rambles coherently about a people who will always have fear and hate those in power. Romantic-Fish has a red splotch near the fish's heart, and I fear Franken-Fish will notice it.

There's a loud banging outside, and I see the neighbors. Mostly everyone relies on screens for any advice, and as a source of entertainment. The neighbors are no different. I am given ideals by my visions, and by my mother, whom I trust, and the doctor, and a few visitors to the split foyer. All assure me that the technological rise is a way to stop people like our stupid neighbors from mindlessly going about in destructive patterns, like savages with too much power driving carelessly and wrecking too many cars.

"Everything is pretty safe," says mother. "Most people don't bother us, but there are always a few." She introduces me to a couple of visitors that have gathered at the doctor's home, for his advice on various conditions is knowledge that is surely in deficit today, and since he is constantly studying medical textbooks, he is able to divvy-out some of his knowledge to people who might need it. His visitors often seek advice from a person instead of seeking help from the automated health continuators, which are available for free in nearly every town square around the world. You just walk into the health surplus pod, and the machines diagnose the best treatment options for your circumstances in one of their germ-free, self-cleansing biohazard pods.

"We wish we didn't need to keep them so complacent," says one visitor. "The damned fools get whatever luxuries they want, until it's time, then we put in earplugs to block the sounds of nocturnal cleansing."

Scientists on Earth had met with the most advanced artificial technology. Super-computers that thought ahead like chess masters were capable of attaining actual consciousness! Soon after the meeting between conscious robotics and highly esteemed humans came the rewards of naturalized citizenship, and the new citizen must have felt like acting like such a responsible citizen should, by getting involved in making decisions. Together, they decided to institute suggested curfews when atmospheric cleansing is necessary, employing the help of human engineered, artificially intelligent, mega-efficient, self-sustaining lunar-powered cleaners.

"So while every idiot is laughing at comedies, and tiring themselves at their chosen jobs," says the visitor to the foyer, "our team has to rework solutions to keep our planet running like it should."

FOUR

A Requiem for My Friend's Farm

"Confounded! Confronting
my sudden realizations.
My eternal self
    drawn into this form.
Drawn into this lie.
What a lie! I recall
    that ancient harmony.
What bitter sounds
    of the end
    of a cold day.
The endless rotation
    like two planets
    my lids won't
    close for long
    not long enough for sleep
    to come.

I must live with the curse.
We, and I,
      will fit our feels to verse."
            —Shane Sullivan

The doctor's daughter visited the infirmary today. That's what we call the lower level now. Anyway, she's a scientist. Says she's been working with me through it all. She admires my poetry too. In fact, she even referred to me as a *word scientist*.

I felt eternity. I feel it again when I look into her eyes. When tiresome fingers fall still, bring me back to eternity, so sayeth thy heart. She looks at me in that old familiar way, and I know she's been through it all with me.

Yet she's involved with another, a Younker from York. I don't know him but I don't care. I found out she was nursing me through it all. Her name sounds familiar, but the way she pronounces it and pretends she's the same as all the rest of us is something brand new. Yet, much of my past has escaped me.

Her words escape her. I feel them all around. Meanwhile, my words escape me in wholesome poetry:

> *Oh budding rose, let's not forget thee*
> *Amidst glorious rising machinery.*
> *Your crescent petals sway our insides*
> *Pulling with nightly force that moves tides.*

> *Your swaying branches, oh wise oak tree,*
> *Now hang forever between matrimony*
> *Of Man and machine. How you witness their lust,*
> *For man to love Woman until she show rust.*

> *He'll beat her and she'll kick him like a dog.*
> *He'll clean her boots with his most precious silk.*

When they melt to a lovely mindless fog,
Who knew the two would yield a mother's milk?

And people love machines no matter the cost.
Shortened seasons and clouds of smog.
Farmers wield causes forgotten and lost.
All hustle without hearing what troubles the hog.

Hearts bend for Forgotten Farms' seclusion.
Mine wavers in endless confusion.

. . . .

The Forgotten Farm Shan't Be Forgot

Ashley's family's farm once shined.
Crowded greenhouses have declined.
Rich corporations gain capital,
While Ash's father must sell off his shovel.

Let us not forget the working party's plight
To live off the land and work with their hands.
The Forgettes Family toiled for what was right,
Centuries of life over limb to meet demands.

The eldest Forgettes man proves exemplary
Of what comes of man's merger with machinery.
The bailer he worked came back to work him
When its growling hunger chopped off a limb.

81

Malin Forgettes never complains
When his hook for a hand causes delays:
Opening cans and x-ray machines.
For it was worth it to his family he says.

But for elders and young ones
Whether they're Forgettes or not,
Must now duck down, below crass company guns.
Man's greed and machine's speed can never be forgot.

. . . .

Mother pulls me up from the infirmary and sees to it that I'm well enough to care for myself. I tell her I am all right and pack my belongings, some drawings and sketches of the world I must learn, and a book filled with my own hieroglyphics.

Valentine fetches my bag, and I notice how he lingers on my notebook longer than I expected. His temperament is coarse, as he runs his hands along the top of his grey hair. It bounds back in shape in a snap.

"Technically speaking, you weren't dead," Valentine says. "You were still alive in a deep sleep. Life support made my job easy. Though I could bring back the dead, I suppose."

"Could you really?" I ask him.

"I could but I don't know if my daughter could help in the way she helped you." He flips through poetry that I had written since my stay began a week ago. I've been writing as a way to let my soul be free, without judgments over any tormented thoughts, and without drawing in spirits (liquor). I haven't touched the wine in days, and the illusions have become seldom.

My latest poem spells out my desires:

A Poet Near the Door of Doom

Here on a page my soul does live,
Occupation as a declaration.
Heaving words to force others to forgive,
Beyond bodily emancipation.

Somehow I survive deathly fires.
Now thoughts mismatch modern desires.
In sleep I found simplicity,
Near Heaven's gate for eternity.

Where does a poem find dreams?
Imagine my muse forever and free,
Lovely gestures pursue requiems,
Lyrical breath for humanity.

Nothing, never, all that I'd know
Without her touch I am shadow.

. . . .

He gets through the drudge I wrote in my stigma and smiles politely at me before shaking my hand.

"This couplet at the end . . . . You are smitten," says Valentine. His anxiety shows terribly.

"I think so," I say with a shameful smirk. "At least I'm honest."

"Stay humble," he says, "those feelings might get you through the darkness you feel surrounding you. Feelings for my daughter?"

"They are," I say. "She's all that I know."

"I understand," he says. "Well, I should say, with caution, reserve those ideas of infatuation for someone else."

"I'll try," I say, but he can tell it's a lie.

"It's typical," says the doctor, "to develop feelings for one's caregiver. Your amnesia bleeds into your sobriety. Don't get lost in the winds of your emotions. She sat with you while you slept, out of pity for the burned poet from Woodlawn. And because I asked her to, she held your hand. But my daughter is betrothed. You must understand, and you must respect this factly matter."

"Yes," I say, "I will." I try to leave in a way that I can stay calm, and undetected, but I can't get out without jeering over the outside world.

FIVE

For the Love of Life Leave Me Alone

Machines make soils churn.
Burning through dirt and decay,
They make their metals earn,
For Jay Hedges: a feast.
But while he's chewing foods
He's overcome by a non-mechanical mood
Of what if he has too much for just himself,
Yet enough for one seems never enough.
                    —*The Hedges*, issue no. 36

Weeks went by when I didn't hear from the doctor, but his daughter came to check on me a few times. She brought canned goods and fresh water when acid rain seeped into the well and turned our water brown. I began to question the meaning of my being brought back to consciousness with relentless curiosity. My visitor became impressed by my stability and ability to refuse the beverage offered to ease my situation.

I became comforted only by the discomforts, those that seemed to match my pain. Lilloo became my unattainable object. I was so enlightened by this discovery that I started to see clearly the reasons for loving the woman, and understand the feelings behind loving whom I once found ludicrous to behold. The beauty and light pouring from a woman's soul kept me sane. I finally understood what

Dante was talking about in *La Vita Nuova*. What he found captivating in his darling Beatrice, I found in Lilloo, and such pains caused me to starve my writing until I could find relief.

I felt the pain without numbness. Beautifully wretched, gut-bursting pain. Pain that wouldn't let me be, but I wasn't asking it to leave me, for I was feeling alive. Acute stinging sensations plagued my being. Those I did not share with her. I couldn't shake the feeling of everything being an illusion presented to me. But this type of illusion was different than the others I had experienced and I've expressed thus far. This type was joyful.

I loved the way she tempted me, but I knew she was reserved, and I felt my own jealous nature sneaking up. She was tempting me for a purpose, thought I. That purpose I found to be better dismissed rather than experienced. That woman's manipulation of my emotions, or my spirit if that exists, was beginning to thwart my recovery.

But what were her purposes of manipulating my emotions? All I knew was that such manipulation was surrounded by pity for me as a confused creature and as a man starving for a beautiful woman's affections. I dismissed the doctor's daughter for good by telling her, finally:

"I want to make advances upon you," said I.

"You do?" she asked, but she wasn't afraid of me like I thought she would be.

"It's not my nature to be so pushy," I said, flinging myself at her being.

"I understand," she resisted. "But it is natural to have those feelings." Though she was younger than I, I felt her emotional intelligence had bested mine, so I pleaded with her to leave.

"If you don't go," I said, "I'll tell you how much I love you. I'll write more and more poetry in your honor. And I'll die with a poisoned heart, but not as lovers seldom do—I'll die a lonely old man. Leave me now. Will you? Will you leave me while I'm still young?" I asked her the favor. "So that I may grow old to love again."

She didn't love me. She cared for me more than anyone ever had though. She cared for me more than I could comprehend. More than I had ever cared for another. More than I knew it was possible to care. For, people are fickle and my health was poor. I could have keeled over and died there in my burned-up apartment.

But she came to me in that tomb that was the worst place I had ever lived, and she cared for me like someone you love. And I sent her away. I'd go on living that way for weeks, alone and without necessities most people figure are needed for life. I withered because I couldn't care for life without love.

Lilloo was born a week early, not premature by any means, but her birth was enough of a shock to give great trouble to her mother. The way the world works isn't always convenient for everyone.

There was a car outside already. Waiting. Full of all the supplies they would need for a natural birth. Mr. & Mrs. Valentine had prepared to visit a field outside of town where the flying robotic machines only visited on weekends. Back then, the dispute over new technologies was less of an issue, since those machines were still being piloted by a human component. The raids outside of the cities were nearly nonexistent, next to none.

Natural birth was preferred in place of the standard of using automated health machines. The conscious class has always preferred natural birthing in place of the other more popular method of sterile birthing pods.

They had the car prepped with clean, fresh linens and towels, a pop-up tent that Sonny had practiced assembling already, and enough supplies to live on the land until it was safe to return to their home. They were all ready to go before Lilloo showed up early.

The sudden shock was too much to deal with, however. Traffic patterns were abnormally heavy that afternoon. The crisp autumn weather hadn't helped when their car stalled out on a turnpike. Rows and rows of cars passed by the trapped family as Mrs. Valentine screamed in pain. Sonny hadn't started training in medical or anatomical medicine yet, so he relied strictly upon his knowledge of the human condition to calm his wife in her final moments.

The last images of life that Mrs. Valentine had experienced were notably bleak, and meaningless. Though, before she died she heard her baby girl crying, so at least she knew she was healthy. She held Dr. Valentine's hand, and forced him to hold their daughter as she bled out entirely.

He soothed the screaming baby and curled next to his wife in the worst pain of being alive. He could feel his wife leave. Her body went limp on the backseat, as her eyes drifted from staring at the endless stream of metal vehicles being operated by people that would not turn from their screens, no matter what was happening around them.

SIX

Lilloo's Circle and Upbringing

Growing up in a small town full of people who have emotions perhaps controlled by some form of robotic simulation proved opportunitious for those conscious folk. Those who could control themselves could meet and mingle among the razor sharp social circles in Woodlawn's Valley Fjord. Lilloo's social circle wasn't filled with merely conscious simpletons, but her peers were highfalutin intellectuals as well, which I was not.

I observed them from the outside with my ruffian group of friends, however. Valley Fjord High School was where I met Ashley Forgettes, Cassandra Spalding, and Travis Frack. We sat together at our own lunch table, and together we sat in most classes. We were seldomly joined by another child, neither the conscious type, nor straying tech-head. We could all hear the technology pouring from their brains with their lousy *video-songs* that would sweep away any teen angst we could have collectively drummed up against our own social circles.

The four of us were bound to each other like a beryllium atom, which has four electrons in its outer shell. However, unlike the beryllium atom, the four of us loved being outdoors in the Valley Fjord. For, the fjord was rich in oxygen. Yet, we mimicked the way the beryllium atom combined to form toxic substances. In this way, we moved together throughout the halls and classrooms. The teachers noted us, how we were creative types. We became known throughout the school as fringe teenagers, with torn jeans, beaded necklaces, spikey hair, colorful clothing, and without being sucked into the consuming technology that swept throughout the majority of our peer groups. Teachers gave us special assignments and duties to assist them in contributing to the programming that would feed the video screens for our classmates.

The other group of conscious teenagers that Lilloo was a part of were more magnificent, like neon, for neon's atomic number is ten, and ten is a perfect number. Human beings have ten fingers, ten toes, and ten is the basic unit in the metric system for a good reason, one should suppose. Neon has ten electrons, and it glows bright orange, so I watched them from the outside to see if I could spot the bright orange enigma. How they loved to preen and tend to their appearances was beyond my understanding. How they patiently waited while being preened by another in their group was beyond my capacity for truly comprehending that certain virtuosity. The girls with their make-ups and eye shadows, especially Lilloo and her purple glaze, impressed the boys they strolled with, who kept neatly combed forehead puffs of hair.

It's a miracle that Lilloo could leave behind that tendency to preen and glaze her appearance as an adult. Perhaps she left it behind due to the manner in which she would spend her time after the mandatory classroom programming. She would ride the bus like the rest of our class, but she'd sit with the other neons, of course. Her circle and my circle, we'd triumphantly speak over the obvious noisemakers with their programmed entertainment machines. They were the randomly charged electrons that floated about incoherently.

One day in particular I can remember the vibrations of their devices overwhelming my senses, and distorting my finely balanced equilibrium. We were close to Ashley's stop, and mine was going to be up shortly. When Ashley left, I was sitting by myself, with

Cassandra and Travis not far away across the aisle. That was when an unconscious twit sat down next to me. Eric had been listening to his device with earplugs, running tiny speakers to project sound to each side of his chubby, contained face. I wasn't worried about or disturbed by him sitting next to me, since he was in his virtual entertainment lifestyle. One of the earplugs must have fallen out from his ears because he turned to me to ask about a peculiar orange substance that had arranged itself in globular formations around the plug.

That was when I took to leaving the bus early for once. That was when I found out more about Lilloo's life. Moreover, I found hints of secrets I deserved to know about my own upbringing, and I would eventually find those out years later when I was reconstructed by Lilloo's father's own invention.

"Hey man, you look worse than you normally do," said Travis Frack, as the bus slowed down. He tried to jostle me with one of his awkward social comments: "You normally look so tired I used to think you were Chinese."

"I need to leave," I said to my friend and covered my mouth.

"Is he Chinese?" Cassandra asked.

"He might have eaten some bad sushi," I heard Travis say before I forced my way off the bus near Lilloo's street.

In between bouts of vomiting in the hedges I overheard Lilloo greeting her father before he left with her bound to his work. She hopped in the same car she was born in actually. He played classic rock, and I saw his car's bumper and trunk were lined with stickers of his favorite bands and radio stations. Grateful Dead bears walking between AC/DC lightning bolts, and a sticker of the lips and tongue of the Rolling Stones.

The next week I had grown accustomed to a few bands from my mother's record collection before I spotted Dr. Valentine's car once more. The windows were down all the way, as he backed up from a spot in front of his office with dear Lilloo in the passenger seat.

The radio disk jockey's voice lifted from the air waves to fill the streets with a form of adult programming: "This is Lopez from our soundstage on Television Hill reminding you to live, laugh, and love." They were headed home after Dr. Valentine wrapped up his experiments for the day. He was fast at work publishing his series of articles that would be slandered as pseudo-science, until after he provided enough evidence to substantiate the development of emotional reasoning for artificially intelligent cyborgs. Lilloo was already helping the cause, keeping his work relevant by weighing in on his writings after school. I knew that much already. So I just figured that she was the main reason he was able to project to such large audiences, and tap into their emotions completely.

I figured then that Lilloo was the reason Dr. Valentine was able to mount a project that is still to this day an attempt to bridge the gap between humans and machines. The project is intended to bring people like Eric into using their devices for the betterment of all. But to go that far, the doctor had to break into a grey area of science, and trample upon the ethics of many others. Types, like he, carefully painted moral ambiguity to be nothing more than a fine line drawn in the sand. Lucky for me, I happened to be swept away by a tide on the beach near where he drew that line. I returned to the shore so that I might help avoid more drownings at sea, so to speak. When I fell in, however, good and evil of humanity and technology fought for me.

When I slipped away, I can't remember machines saying much at all on the otherside. When I slipped in, I didn't know how they fought to obtain my being. When they took me from the fires and brought me back in secret, there was resistance. Where there is resolution, there was once desolation.

Now, I fear what evil will catch me alive and well.

SEVEN

A Confession Signed

I t wasn't always a plan. It was never something we talked about, but the bullying manner and the peering eyes were too much to handle, I suppose. And I suppose, a boy always needs to defend his mother, and a mother—a good mother, which she was being—should put the world underground to keep her son safe from harm. Without admonishing too greatly, I remember dear Praxilla, who wrote warnings of such in her epigram titled *The Cowards*. Of those who cloak themselves, and attack us from any direction, she wrote such advice for us: "Watch out for his sting. Under every rock is a scorpion."

In the end, you'll understand why I can no longer claim to be the innocent man I thought I once was. Yet, for, it is human nature to fight for one's own survival. For safety and survival, we fight for what we believe to be right, and sometimes we must fight to the death for it. What is in our control is whether or not we choose nature over nurture. And I must plead guilty in choosing nature.

Looking back on how I've arrived here, I've never had it easy when I thought about making friends, and that goes the same before I was brought back from the deep sleep caused by fires. In my early era, when I was a young man of age seven I suppose, I switched private schooling systems due to an obsessive, abusive teacher. She was the type of teacher who would hold a student's mouth and force the child's jaw to move if she caught the child refraining from saying the words to a pledge. I found this out the hard way when I did not willingly recite the words of our school's patriarch mascot, St.

Timothy, a man who rarely, if ever introduced himself to us children. My impression of god had came to me without the saint, so I felt little obligation to pay my respects to him, and I would refrain from doing so on my own free volition. As if having a class full of obedient children, good natured children, wasn't enough, the forced recitation of a pledge mustn't have subdued her ego either, so she got off feeding our class pictures of abortions. Such pictures would ruin our youthful smiles forever. These events lead to the first significant time my mother came to my side as my defender.

But to be fair, mother already had a habit of showing her good nature without being called upon when her son cried for help. One time, she came to school to pick me up before the buses took away the other children, all wearing starched shirts, khaki pants, and shiny leather shoes or boots. Autumn wasn't making it easy for us to play in the fields. The leaves were piled, and we got into horrendous fights over who's turn it was to swing the baseball bat at the fence to knock down more acorns from a nearby tree. The chain-link fence had caused our cheap plastic bat to dwindle, and that deficiency gave room for mother to enter, even with a simple modest provision. She was the hero.

After all, my father taught me about keeping my eye on the ball and what direction I had to run after swinging for it from home plate, but mother showed me how to make friends with my teammates. She set such an example that was impossible for me to follow, one autumn day after classes were complete, while we were running around outside of St. Timothy's Academy, playing some odd, childish game; we made up the rules. My team had collected the most acorns already and there weren't many left, but Owen was up at bat, and oh boy, could he swing! When Owen ran, even my mother had to watch the way his hands seemed to cup at the air, and, as he pulled his body through it, his ankles took him to new heights along his destination. The teams were tied after Owen ran around banging on the fence before getting tagged like the rest of us. Mother saw how friendly I was getting along with the boys there. Oh, how they cheered me on, and how I actually had my own best friend for the first and only time, ever in my life.

Ben was brilliant in his studies, but he wasn't good at sports, mainly because his parents couldn't afford to buy him a proper mitt to catch fly balls, so he held out a thin gardening glove that usually caved in when the ball came near. That earned Ben a black-eye one day. My mother must have heard that story a dozen times, so I wasn't shocked when she brought Ben a present that day, when we played under the acorn tree.

It was Ben's turn to run for the fence with the broken plastic bat. When the first acorn fell from the tree, my mother joined him in "collecting the candy from nature's piñata," and calling out a childish rhyme while playing.

Tree nuts!
Acorn landy.
Tree, can you?
Drop more candy!

That was when she gave the gift to Ben she had bought and kept hidden in the cool front trunk of her Italian sports car.

She picked up acorns and filled the glove before she passed the entire lot to my oldest best friend, Ben. She was pleased to find out that Ben liked the glove right then and there.

"Would you wish it to be yours?" she asked.

"I would, ma'am," Ben said politely.

She gave him the thick leather glove, along with a new foam bat. The bat was green with a black handle, and Ben left that old, chewed up yellow bat in the dirt when he ran back to home base with the loot, not long before the other team came to tag him out.

"You'll make other friends," said mother when she found out from me about the abusive teacher. The rumor that she was keeping children who disobeyed her in her closets was downright hard to believe, even for my young mind, but the fact that she was hardened and cruel enough to take a little boy's face in her hands (like she knew better than I what words should've been coming from my own mouth), was enough for mother to keep a close eye on my studies. When she found out that the teacher was showing us disturbing images, her natural inclination was to take the complaint to the pulpit before she pulled me from that school altogether. I moved from St. Tim'thy to St. Paul's Academy almost immediately. So long to the first friends I had made on my own, and so long to my first best friend I ever did have. He wasn't the same ethnicity as I, so there wasn't much in common to bring us together as friends, said the adults, except a universal desire: to be liked and accepted by another of our own peers. I liked having my friend Ben from St. Tim's. He was the first person outside of my relatives to give a damn about me, but he knew to never get too close. Some people get too close to things they shouldn't look into, and that's why I must confess to the dark deeds we've done.

It wasn't hard to make friends in the next private school, yet perhaps it was only easy because mother introduced me to the scene, as she sat at the long lunch table with me on the morning of the first day. She had worn her hair fashionably spiked, and her shirt even had a collar still on it. The children at the lutheran school ushered in before seven o'clock to sit with their respective grades, and on such occasion they found my mother sitting there waiting to introduce me to their class, characters with whom I would become thoroughly acquainted with in the coming years. There was Lancie, the dumb bully who would turn out to be a loyal friend to us all in the end— Andrew whose family ran a strange religious camp that excited children's curiosities (with a truly fascinating rope swing that glided into a mattress that was mounted on an oak tree at the end of a zipline), and like a prospective saint, Andrew could read quicker than anyone—There were two girls who were best friends, each with strongly different lives: one the daughter of a prince from Cameroon, and the other was from a broken home. All these children seemed plain to me at first, perhaps because I was frightened. So I rocked in that orange plastic chair, shifting my weight back onto its thick wire-frame legs, doing enough posing to feel cool and rebellious because I felt like I could get away with being bad before mother left.

"Stop," said mother. She told them all who I was, "This is Shane. He's cool." She convinced the kids that I wasn't too tough or strange because I came in like the wind, in November, to join them for forced study. I can remember Andrew believing her, but it might have been my doing when I rocked back in the chair the way I did.

. . . .

98

We made friends that day, thanks to mother, and I make more friends today because of her still, perhaps. But I must sadly report that the man whom I have crossed in the dark deeds I have committed was not a friend of mine a'tall, even though I lied and told my mother he was a dear old friend.

Detective Richard "Richie" Hoake remembered me from kindergarten. The only year of primary school of which I attended an institution in the public school system was when we met. I rode the bus and laughed with the other children, about cartoons and where our parents were born. Meanwhile poor Richie was over there by his lonesome without any friends to sit with on the bus. Richie was caught picking his nose excessively, on more than one occasion, and, for some reason the booger-flicker always wanted to sit next to yours truly. My situation was immediately improved when the other children on the bus showed me how to put my feet onto the seat in front of me, which temporarily stopped Richie from joining me. I didn't want to be his friend, and quickly grew tired of him trying to be mine, so I made up a little lie to tell my mother about Richie being a bus bully.

"He's the one who keeps picking on me," I whined to her.

She told me that I'd never have to ride the bus again. She told me she'd talk to Richie's mother and make sure he got what he deserved. I didn't hear from Richie at primary school again. I assumed nothing, oblivious through my childish existence, until Richie caught up with me when we were grown men.

To be honest, I didn't realize it was him, since his coat looked so clean, and his fingers weren't grubby. His hands were kept cleaner than mine own around the cuticles and under his nails. I could tell the officer at my door wasn't much older than I. He wouldn't give me his badge number or his last name, and I could tell he was lying when he told me to call him Eddie, but I went along with it.

"I've been watching you," said the detective. "You were badly burned," he said. He looked surprised. "Now you walk among everyone else. You should be sick in bed, but you're alive. But how is that?"

"It's a miracle," I claimed, "that my muscles grew stronger, and the flesh leapt right over where the flames had left off."

"You're unholy!" the detective yelled and cornered me in the ally. I slipped up the fire escape, but when I crossed the rooftops and made my way down the neighbor's ladder, I could see the badge was waiting down below.

"I bet you don't remember," the detective said to me, "but I wanted to be your friend once. That was back before you were a monster. I was a child and wanted to sit next to you and be your friend, but you and the other children shunned me like I was some kind of evil beast."

"Richie?" I asked, knowing it was he.

"When your apartment went up in flames I was called in to help the emergency responders load you into a healing pod," said Richie. "I actually felt bad for you, despite you shunning me when we was kids."

"Well," I said, "kids will be—they'll be those things. They do, you know."

"I know too well," he said. "I brought gifts to your hospital room, palms on the Sunday of the few times I visited you. Your mother didn't remember me neither."

"Well, she's not got a way with faces," I told him.

"But I remember her," he said with gleaming eyes. "I can remember when she came by my family's house after school, to talk to my mother about beating on you."

"I'm sorry about that," I told Richie. "I just wanted to get out of riding the bus, you see. It was a long time ago."

"Eons," said Richie. His eyes lit up under the clear blue skies, and his voice cracked down, like a stone plummeting, over the sound of the running waterfall in the pond out back. "My mother wasn't home. She was at the casino. But my dad was there, wondering where the fuck his dinner was. And when your mother talked to my father about his son's behavior—I haven't picked my nose much lately. Do you know why, Shane?"

"Why not, Rich?"

"Cause every time I touch the fucking thing it bleeds like it did when my old man tried to *correct* my behavior."

"What a shame," I said. I felt extremely uncomfortable, but I tried to play it cool. I actually started to think Richie wanted to be my friend again, like he was reliving some dream he had when we rode the bus together as children. We followed each other around the yard behind the apartment building, around the pond, and over near the lot that links and joins the properties in the back. We were clearing sticks from the yard and enjoying some sunlight when he got too close, and kept prying away at me.

. . . .

"How come you don't look burned?" he asked me. He wouldn't accept my short answers about creams and healing from sunlight. He wouldn't leave me be. He crossed his arms and threatened to put a gun to my head, if I didn't give him answers he thought were honest, he said.

Since the entire situation caught me by surprise, I didn't know what to do. I walked off, but the detective followed me, relentlessly. He never actually let me see his badge, so I figured I was better off not complying with such a rogue. For, I thought he might be a stalking occultist, one of those obsessed types who read 'The Hedges' and wanted my autograph, or I figured he might-as-well be one of those raiders I've been warned about, so I walked off in the general direction of my family's home where my mother lives.

The stately Woodlawn Manor is an old tudor home not far from my apartment. I didn't have the security code memorized, so I sat on the poarch outside. I remember it being white, but the wall near the lattice was coated with layers of paint, like the feathers of a lark, with a metal awning that had its spurs dug like talons above the door. I sat outside the screen door, on the stone steps of the uneven, paved granite rock. That rock was pulled from a nearby quarry when the home was built as a gift for Washington's nephew. The first president of the country didn't have any children of his own, so he built homes for his nieces and nephews around Virginia and Maryland. Some people claim to have seen his ghost riding a white horse around the grounds of Woodlawn Manor.

When the would-be-curious creeping stalker approached me, I took out from my pea coat a deck of fifty-two playing cards that were adorned with gold trim around the edges and had mallard ducks painted on the backs of the cards. The ducks were in mid-flight, and so was I when I saw Richie. I shuffled them between my hands. My flushing of cards was cascading more brilliantly than ever before when the stalker knocked them from my grasp. I stepped to him before my mother came around to the screen door of the kitchen, where she must've seen us through the window.

She asked me if everything was all right, and I said, "Yes, all right, mother. Go inside." I felt safe there, but I truly didn't want to have mother get involved. Truthfully, I did not.

Richie saw the torn neckline of mother's shirt, a style she notoriously adored, and has adorned herself with since I can remember. The stalker switched targets. Just like that then. We were inside the kitchen when I lied to mother by saying that this man was a friend. She knew by the sound of my voice that it was a lie. Motioning for me to come aside, she asked me if we were comparing ourselves by length of flesh, but before I could answer her rude accusation, Richie was in the basement at Woodlawn Manor.

I can't tell what he was looking for. There were all kinds of rumors about the Manor being haunted, since the actual plantation was built by slave hands. A scholar once said: "Those that work to the bone never leave—Those muscles and bones that toil to no end, and for the profit of keeping up another family's household, without the ability to freely be—They keep permanent stations, arranged even in the afterlife." I had also feared he was searching for the doctor, or would find one of those strange machines that were used to reconstruct my injured body.

My mother tended to the wash nearby as Richie peeped at the crevasses around the basement, looking for any clue, I suppose. He was near the corner of the wall by the door that leads out to the tarmac driveway. In that corner, as he stooped down to inspect the area, I saw an unfinished portion of the Manor's frame was sticking out sharply, protruding as if it had never been refined after all those years of entertaining parties in the basement. It struck me as odd that all the hands that crafted the estate hadn't occupied themselves with taking away this one sharp hunk of metal that stuck out from the wall. But I've always known there was something off about the Woodlawn Manor. The lights in the master bedroom turn on by themselves. Things fall from the shelves in the dining room all by themselves, and you can often hear a thumping sound, much like the wooden peg-leg of a wounded soldier, moving across the floorboards. It may have been the bloodshed that brought devastation to Woodlawn, or the mistreated souls that still hang out in the ether, breathing cold air along your neck when you least expect it. Whatever it was, and for whatever reason it may be, that jagged piece of the Manor's skeleton was left alone for all those years! So I took it as a sign, to push Richie into it, when he knelt down close to the rusty shrapnel.

Thwack!

His head flopped like an apple on a pike as it stuck to the rusted metal scrap the first time I pushed him into it. He peeled himself from the trap like a fly might have life enough left to spring from glue, after first landing. He tried to make another crass comment about my mother, but his brain was badly damaged from that first traumatic hit. He was trying to change the world, but he was all by himself in our basement. He took a hit, yet, still, he didn't show much pain for all the blood he was losing. I take it that Richie liked taking risks; perhaps he was the extremely dangerous type of detective because he moved like a predator, to get to my mother. He advanced on her, so I took him out at the knees, like my father had taught me. When he laid on the floor moaning in agony, I finally bashed his head good.

Richie's strong build might've been helpful getting him through the physical agility test, to get into the academy, but he lacked proper judgment, and perhaps he became personally invested in my case, as well. I expected the skull to quickly cave from the corrupted blows on the Manor's hard cement, but it held together, long enough for mother to have to help me in finishing the disturbing deed I started.

By the end of it all, we could have done no worse to Richie if he were a mouse sealed in a plastic bag. We put his body in the cool front trunk of mother's Italian sports car.

"I thought you sold this thing eons ago," I said. We hid the car, and we hid his squad car too.

There are important matters at hand, so all mannerisms that stand to unite humanity and technology are for the good of all. We have been called to attend to such matters, and I think Richie was becoming too privy to our goings-ons. I would be so bold as to speculate that he was looking for a way to upset our intentions.

Either way, I know it is my doing, and I accept full responsibility for killing this man.

EIGHT

Slipping Away: Reality's Grip

The oppressive woman with short hair and glasses came from the art room that day. She was covered in clay. She stomped around in strapped flats and knee-high socks that concealed most of her flesh from clay and other foul substances.

"Her feet must stink," Ben suggested to me and the other boys, while we waited for the bell to ring.

"All the way down in those socks must be the smelliest part of the world."

At the school's library, we were working in groups to create presentations on the most extreme places around the world. My group searched for information on the driest desert in all the lands, which turns out to be in South America. A place called the Atacama Desert still holds that title. It's along the coast of South America in a climate that not too many people would choose to remain. Mining operations have caused the water supply in the small town of Quillagua to become poisonous to its people, so there was a need for scientists from the mining company to intervene. This type of research would usually cause me to work up an appetite, but this time it made me so thirsty that I asked for water and permission to visit the fountain down the hall. My stomach was aching, so I thought some water might help it settle.

When I returned to the library, I found my friends had decided to take time away from doing their assigned research, and they were instead roaming about the small library. Noisily, they were doing their own research. They were looking at books of bugs and bacteria when I found them. Tim and Owen laughed aloud as Ben walked around with his socks rolled up, over his pant cuffs, like Mrs. Flap, our second grade teacher.

They showed me the picture in the book they were holding when I asked for it. They didn't force me to look at the pictures of fungus that grows and is found on peoples' feet. They didn't force me to think about how horribly itchy it must feel. They didn't make me watch them take a knife to somebody's toes to peel it away. They were doing their own research, and we shared our findings about the world with one another, as young gentlemen may do.

"I bet Flap's feet are worse off than that," I said. I took their book and flipped through it.

"Worse than what?" asked Mrs. Flap. She moved around the bookshelves with intensity I had never witnessed in a library before. Her socks were higher than Ben's. He adjusted his footwear, as I slammed the book closed. We left back to our assigned groups before she could punish us.

The very next day I noticed Ben wasn't present at school. Owen and I looked for him at recess. His house was close enough that we went by and found out his mother kept him home from school. She told us how their family was very strict, and Ben was in big trouble for what he did making fun of Mrs. Flap's feet.

We made it back before the bell, "hell's bell" according to Owen, and we made it to class on time. Flap prepared a special presentation for us to see. "Instead of having each of your groups discuss what you found out about the world yesterday," said Flap, "in the library. Instead, I'd like to show you what is really going on in other parts of the world. You're all getting older and need to know the truth about what is out there!" She was frowning, and her bottom teeth showed while she said, "It is my job to show you."

Our second grade class sat silently, as the teacher took time to spread her ideals, like Plato with his talk on a thief, but the shipwrecked man was me, and Flap's sea of torment stripped me of everything I held dear. "This is what the church believes," she would later say in her own defense. The pictures she showed were sill-hou-ettes, making the figures look like blobular cartoon characters instead of realistic people. The details of what the cartoons were doing left much to the imagination. As we watched her flip through and explain what was happening in each picture, our minds were able to fill in the gaps of what the pictures weren't showing.

Our innocent, untamed imaginations became the breeding ground for her staunched ideals, those that wrecked our young minds belonged best in a fiery pulpit church sermon, or perhaps they should have been reserved for politicians to discuss on television shows that broadcast to all our ears night and day, like 'The Hedges' surely does. Or perhaps such life decisions should be kept sacred for each individual to discuss when they are ready. Flap, like Plato's thief character, "was ashamed to strip me of my last garment." Our ship went through hazardous storms of which we hadn't known possible, until at last we were washed up on our own individual island, making use of our mental fortitudes to cope with a terribly lonely feeling of uncertainty. Myself, as well as the rest of my class, could tell what was going on in those pictures even though none of us children had once witnessed an abortion before. Not one of us had ever had the idea of what it would be like to see a living thing cut from another living thing and left for dead.

Any person that tries to contest the ability to program a child by showing images and over-exposing a young mind, anyone who denies behaviorism, and to any individual who argues that we are not the product of our own environments— Just ask any of us what we think of abortion.

Later on, after school, I tried hard to avoid telling Ben what we learned about from Flap's anti-abortion pictures for all ages presentation. Instead, I tried asking him what the teacher told his mother about his behavior, and why he was punished. But I had some trouble focusing on listening about anything at all. I couldn't get those cartoon blobs out of my head.

"What's wrong, Shane?" asked Ben.

"I got something in my head that I don't want there," I said. I couldn't get those blobs out of my head no matter how hard I tried to forget, so I told my friend to keep a secret, even though I didn't want them to be in his head either. I didn't know what to do; they looked like they were in such great pain and torment.

Undoubtedly, Ben's mother must have overheard me telling her son about the way the cartoon people were cutting open a lady to remove the baby she didn't want. I know she heard me telling Ben because she asked me to tell my mother when she came to pick me up, but my stomach was hurting too bad to talk about what I saw. Not to them anyhow.

They were ladies, so I figured they might feel even worse than I felt about what we were learning. That was the last time I saw Ben. We always used to talk about how different we were from each other, since our skin colors weren't the same and our hair grew-in differently, but we'd always forget about that and lose track of time. Running around in grass, looking for bugs in the yard. I even let Ben take the first swing at the real piñata on my birthday.

"Two bugs in the same jar have to be friends, or else one bug will swallow up the other one," Ben realized and said to me one day. Neither of us got eaten, but I was glad we weren't bugs, even if we were to be friendly bugs that wouldn't dare eat one another. I was thankful for being a boy and not a bug.

My stomach stopped aching when my mother pulled me from the school and away from Mrs. Flap's instructions. The images of the cartoons, I was told, would fade away eventually, but they are still present, somewhere, in my mind's-eye, today.

I missed the friends I had made, and even though I started getting along with the children at a new school, it wasn't the same. I felt that I was having something taken away from me. By the time I reached St. Paul's my old friends felt like distant memories already, existing in the same place as those pictures Mrs. Flap said were representing "a miracle being taken away." I went on for years believing abortion to be evil, and I thought anyone engaged in it would be sent straight to hell. For, I thought I understood and knew what loss was about from losing contact with young friends. After my friends were flushed out of my system, thanks to a teacher who was afraid to show her own skin, I thought I knew what loss was.

My grades dropped to failing and I became sullen and sad. "I hate my life," I told my mother, in tears, because I didn't have the friends I grew up to love any longer. Mother came up with an idea to throw a party, and we invited all the neighborhood children over to play board games, and play with model trains. Ben was invited too. But he never made it. There weren't many other children in my neighborhood, so the party ended up being terrible. I was the sad little boy sitting in his basement with his dogs and his trains.

My imagination started running wild, however. I started pretending I was a cowboy with two Appaloosas, and a Quarter-horse instead of two Labradors and a German shepherd. Imagining that my dogs were horses was one way that I coped with loss. The imagination does plenty to get us through stressful events. To me, I had three horses and we were riding near trains in the Old West. I wasn't alone for long, however. I was the sheriff of the town, when one of the most dangerous outlaws in all the land had appeared.

In reality, that was when a neighbor showed up. He was older than I, and he wasn't a real outlaw by typical standards. But I heard plenty of stories about the uninvited party guest stealing motorcycles and cutting the heads off the neighborhood farmer's chickens. Mother didn't know he had snuck in, but I spotted him outside before he came in through those swinging doors; he had been hanging from a tree in the yard like an orangutan. The uninvited party guest always hung around in the tree next to Woodlawn Manor, and he'd spy on its occupants. I found him in the oak one day while he was peeping on my mother, and I told him he'd better not come back my way again. But he had snuck in that day to try to cheer me up when my party wasn't going as planned. He brought a few presents along with him:

"Open the box," said the guest.

"Why'd you bring mice?" I said. "We don't need more pets."

"They're not as pets," he said with a smile. "Pick one of them out, Shane."

I didn't know what he had planned, but I thought that he was onto something fun, perhaps a magic trick even. So I pointed at one of the cute fluffy creatures in the cardboard box. The mouse I pointed at had red eyes and a tiny furry tail. "That one's cute," I told him. He picked that mouse up by its tail, holding it high, high enough for the mouse to look down on the party guest.

"You're the lucky one," the guest told the mouse. That mouse had stopped looking to us for explanation and started curling up towards the guest's fingers. She took a bite out of the guest's thumb, and she fell to the ground, in a run already, after the guest dropped her onto the hard floor.

"Looked like she might have hurt her leg," I said, trapping the mouse between a toy train and the basement wall.

"Look at how fast she runs," said the neighbor, "even with that broken foot."

"Do you think her foot is broken for real?"

"Probably so," he said. He picked up the train, and he held the mouse there with his hand. "You afraid if I let her go? Seeing as she runs fast she might get away in your house."

"So what? It's just a mouse."

He let the mouse free to run and explore the crevasses of the basement of Woodlawn Manor on its own. "Here's the other," said the uninvited guest. "Maybe we could keep him from running off in your house. Cause you know, he might meet with that other mouse and have little mouse babies. They'll infest your house. Big time."

That's when the guest opened a plastic sandwhich bag, and he tossed the other furry creature into it. This mouse was a boy, and you know how you could tell. It had black and white spots on it like a cow does. I don't know what prompted the sickness that followed, but the guest tossed the bag across the basement, and it landed on the hard cement floor.

Smack!

The guest walked across the basement and stepped on the bag, crushing the defenseless mouse inside the plastic enclosure. The mouse was still alive in there. It was still moving. It was making the worst sound I'd ever heard, but it stopped making that sound shortly thereafter.

When it stopped crying, I got really close to the bag with my guest. He picked up the bloody bag, but that mouse stayed as still as could be. Its heart was still beating, quickly. It was the worst thing to witness, but it was still happening. "What are you going to do now?" my tiny voice asked, with regard for the dear creature's life.

"Nothing," said the neighbor, and he got up to leave.

"What do you mean? You can't leave this here!"

"You can keep him," said the cruel party guest, before leaving entirely.

There was nothing I could have done for the mouse. I didn't know the first thing about fixing a bone, and up until that very moment I had hardly known anything about what mice had looked like inside. I took something from the shelf next to the washer and dryer in the basement of Woodlawn Manor. My tiny arms held a rusty old pipe. I hadn't any idea where the pipe had come from, but I came across it while playing in the basement one day. It was left over from making the building, I suppose, since I found it in the wall's interior.

113

I thought it might be something to fend off an intruder if there ever was one. When I found it while playing in the basement, I decided to hide that rusty pipe on the shelf where I didn't think anyone else would come across it. Why I didn't leave it in the wall where I found it, I do not know. I suppose it is human nature to prepare to defend oneself.

Looking into those tiny eyes, and, seeing the life-force of another living creature fading away was more than I could bare. I didn't know if it felt pain, and I wanted to stay with it to show it the world wasn't always that violent. I wanted to show it that some creatures care for other creatures. I opened the plastic bag, and I touched its tiny furry head once. I told the mouse, "There's nothing I can do for you. But if you're feeling pain, I can stop it."

I used the pipe to end that poor mouse's life.

When I woke up the next morning, I tried to tell myself it was all a dream, some horrible nightmare. But there was no use, for as hard as I tried, I couldn't convince myself that it wasn't real. It was the way it went, and I'd always have to live with that memory.

I smashed that creature to end its life!

But it was already in such great pain, I tried to reconcile.

I wanted to talk to someone, but I couldn't tell anyone. None of my friends at school could know, or else they might not want to be my friend anymore. I thought Ben would have listened and stayed my friend, but his mother heard me telling about those bad things I learned in class. I would tell the pastor at school, but he'd surely say it was a sin, thought I. More than anything else I was worried about how mother would be disappointed in what I had done.

That's the way it is when I look into a screen today. When I look into the vortex of images and have my memories recreated in front of my eyes. I, along with many others, look into the fish tank and see digital creations of past memories. We feed on these strong emotions. The advanced artificial digital re-creations of former memories have gotten precise. Their goal is to have people dependant. And most people around the world are easily influenced, especially when it comes to feeding strong emotions to their minds.

The digital fish tank must have realized how strongly I felt about the blobular images, how they made my stomach turn at the thought of the pain associated with those past memories from Flap's anti-abortion presentation. The pain the blobular shapes brought to me lit up my face and kept me tuned in to see more of what the fish tank could come up with based on my memories. It found verifiable proof that certain images will likely dictate a similar outcome every time. For, every time I see those blobular forms floating around in a three-dimensional digital display, I feel like someone is cutting a baby from a lady's body. The same way a digital re-creation of a mouse would remind me of the feeling of playing god with a mouse's life.

That's the type of energy my mind fed on when I last engaged with the device in my basement that is a portal to my soul. I haven't looked for evidence of who I am in the digital re-creation since I last tried to fit in with the other kids, and that was years ago, when I was first becoming a teenager. I looked at the tank and felt that same feeding frenzy of violence and disgust of playing GOD to another smaller living thing.

I grew up without screens dominating my life. Although I did eventually try once more to look at the fish tank as a way of finding myself as an adult. That happened after I awoke from the fire's rage. That was after the doctor brought me back from a deep sleep. I looked into the fish tank, and I relived the act of killing again!

It was a joyous feeling! Joy can become fleeting if it pulls from you in the wrong direction. Oh, how fleeting joy was. I looked into the fish tank to feel memories of my childhood recreated for me as if they were happening presently, and, when I did that, the memory processor picked a memory of loss, associated with losing friends in my life, and it used that memory to have me live through the events of killing a man! I finally awoke from the fish tank with that deep memory that I would never forget. I knew who I was. I wasn't a killer, but I have made such choices to simulate what that must be like.

The technology was so engrossing, so entertaining. I was convinced that I had killed a man. I was convinced that my mother had helped me destroy a man who was my enemy. I did not know it was the fish tank that was making me feel these ways, so now, I go from my burned apartment to Woodlawn Manor, to visit my mother's home. When I turned off the screen, it was as if I had turned away from that killer's vision, and that life has since faded away, thankfully. I hadn't murdered a man for looking too closely. The garage is empty at Woodlawn Manor, apart from my mother's white truck. The old Italian sports car is nowhere to be found, ever since it was sold for parts years ago.

I never used those screens for a good reason. I knew they became wildly advanced, and now I know what that's like as an adult. I had slipped away from the grip of reality, but now I am back. I have returned.

116

The tank I was sitting too close to had cleverly created a world for me to believe. Where my guilt for lying about the nosey boy picking on me on the bus had been manipulated before my eyes. I was tricked to believe a false reality for the last time. I now know what to look for to tell the difference, but I needed help gaining control, and I needed to find a way to give back for this gift of being alive again.

It was time to help the world as my payment.

NINE

(No Title Given)

The doctor himself was alarmed at my reports of hallucination, psychosis, and overall occupation with a disjointed, disassociated reality. His daughter had not been by my apartment to visit and check in on me ever since I sent her away. Our connection was stronger than I have ever experienced, far stronger than when we knew each other in high school, before we each fled from our social *sircles* to experience life outside of our predetermined vortexes.

She was beautiful beyond comparison then, and I was overwhelmed, like most of the other boys, by the overwhelming desire to impress her. However, wherever she would go the world seemed to open up to her, and I was just another one of the boys around that longed to get her attention. Lilloo was, as discussed by Plato, much like the beautiful courtesan named Lais, "who kept a swarm of young lovers," and as beauty deteriorated, the legendary Lais no longer wished to see her reflection, so she left her mirror to the goddess of love, and said, "for I will not see myself as I am now, and cannot see myself as I was."

Yet, I speak too soon, for nothing of this lady has withered, and, perhaps, none ever shall! One time in particular, I was with her when our groups intersected for a demonstration outside of classes. We walked in late to a screening event. The demonstration was of a program being developed to assist young children. I thought it was a typical survey in true democratic form, but the developer took

118

over the stage to make further comments about the development of the program when she saw Lilloo was present. Lilloo was asked to come up to join a select group to share with the wealthy audience her own views. They waited patiently to hear what an upper echelon type of woman would think of the program: "I come from but a small family, in the rural lands of Howard's Country," she said to the captive group, "where poverty does not exist because every individual is valued for their own contribution."

Her words went far to inspire developers of the program that day, and they continue to inspire developers of programming used on screens in classrooms today, but she has since become more interested in finding ways to refine the program designed to link social groups. There are distinct differences between the vast majority of peaceful people living among machines and the technophobic raiders that live outside cities.

The doctor visits to observe my obscure habits and lack of activity, and he suggests we run through tests to better understand whether or not I will be able to continue to assist in his experiments. For, both he and Lilloo fear that I may be a danger to myself and to other people, which would warrant strict isolation. For, if I fall into another state of non-reality and convince myself it's happening, I could become violent.

His visit takes place in the afternoon, when the sun is at its mightiest height in the sky above. We sit outside in its warmth, and crunching leaves make nice sounds, welcoming our appearance in the grassy area behind my apartment building. It's a place where people walk their dogs, and make gardens along the fences for vegetables to grow. This is where the doctor has decided to inform me on which tests we'll administer today. We sit out in this calm surrender, as a flying machine moves across the distant horizon, far enough away to sound like a distant swarm of honey bees, as we sit under the trees.

"The first test is to see if you're processing information normally," says Dr. Valentine. (We sit outside after this first test, beginning after his explanation of the entire day's events.) "It's a long day," Valentine says. "No surprises for either of us, okay?" I nod. "Just be aware of the unexpected. You're going to get tired out by the end of it all. I'll stick around to observe you then, I suppose," he says before handing a clipboard to me.

The first tests are a series of general aptitude assessments. Nothing in it is too tough. An average high school graduate wouldn't have doubts along the way. Questions involve either science, math, or reading comprehension. The math portion is by far the easiest part for me to complete, despite the long division and illogical problem solving. The doctor notices how I don't use scrap paper for the longer algebra equation. "You finished quickly. Nine minutes," he congratulates me. "It usually takes most people ninety."

He spends a few minutes taking notes in the sun before we go inside to get away from the growing noise of the flying cleaning machine.

He warned me earlier about the motor skills ability testing portion: "It's more of a test of stamina than strength," he said during the opening explanation.

His briefing was accurate. He has me pick a stationary exercise, a pose or plank to hold. I choose to remain in a falcon balance while Valentine monitors my heart rate. "Unnatural," he says, looking at the steady rate of my ticker. "Most people have this rate at a standstill."

"Well, then what's the big deal?" I ask while keeping my body balanced.

"Mostly because, well, you see," he searches for the right thing to say. "You see it's a normal rate when at rest. I think the rapid ability to recall information and the way your heart seems to never tire, both might be side effects of being charged out of your coma the way you were."

"During the reconstruction," I say. He nods.

The next test is as bizarre as he claimed it would be during the briefing. I sit in a chamber deprived of light and sound, and I am asked to take note of any change that occurs within my sealed container.

The experiment had started off fine enough. Apart from the scent of polyvinyl chloride, plastics that make up the thick walls, ceiling, and floor of the container. A single colored light is rather soothing to watch. In the middle of this space, the light does change from red to blue, from blue to green, and from green back to red again. I record this in my notes, as I was asked to record such observations. I'm writing but the pen I use runs out of ink altogether. So I am yelling for Valentine to assist me in this matter.

But the doctor doesn't hear me inside the chamber. I figure it's been an hour at least already. I figure he might have fallen asleep, or he could have went to get us both lunch, and maybe he's stuck in traffic. Thinking of Valentine stuck in traffic causes me to think about Lilloo. I want to write more beautiful poetries when I think of her radiance. But the pen seems to have clogged. I shake the pen, hoping to unclog the tip and dispel its ink again. Something comes out, but the something that does come out isn't ink, however. It's a granule of sand. I examine the tip and more sand comes from it. It's coming out fast. When I try to stop the flow, it's no use. The sand is filling the room at a greater speed than before. The pen that was once firing sand, arrogantly, at the plastic walls becomes buried in the new dune. The bottomless fountain must pull sand from deserts all around the world. The Sahara. The Atacama. The Mohave. The colors of sand range in color accordingly so. On a positive note, I can no longer smell the sharp stench of plastic. Yet, the dust is rather choking to my flow of air. Finally, I cough and gag. I choke and I sputter. I kick and scream to free myself from the trap I've sprung on the world.

The ceiling raises up enough to allow for me to stand tall in the blinding white light. I feel the doctor's palm touch my shoulder. "You're alright," he says. He shakes me, and as my clothing drops sand from its particles, I know how a dirty rug must feel: I need to be hung on a clothes-line and hit with a broom, until all the sand is gone. I tell him this.

"You're going to be fine," he says. "You're still at home. Tell me what happened in there." I try to explain but it makes no sense to Valentine.

He looked shamefully uncertain when he disclosed the last test during the briefing. "It's only a precautionary test, really. I don't expect to find anything," he said. "This last test I might as well tell you, is to figure out if you got psychic ability."

"If I do?" I asked.

"If you do, we'll have some luck," he said.

"You think this is luck? Last night I was convinced I'd killed a man," I said. "And this morning I was reliving my childhood, years six to twelve."

"That sounds wonderful," he conceded. "Perhaps, if you can do such things, then perhaps we'll have luck raising the dead."

Since we have to start the psychic ability test in a controlled environment, the doctor decides it's worth taking me back to the infirmary with his fish tanks, in the basement of the split-level home. On the way, he assures me, "If you show psychic ability, it'll be clear with this machine I have."

But perhaps Plato wasn't writing simply, about Lais becoming old and refusing to see herself that way. Perhaps we cannot possibly look to ourselves in the past, for the way we looked, and the ideas we had are no longer living as once they were.

He turns a dial and the humming begins. "When you get there in the land of the dead," he says. "I mean, if this works, and if you get there. You'll be in control of who we're bringing back from the dead. That's a big responsibility, you know. I mean, it will be when you do—"

I think for a moment but the answer is already clear to me.

TEN

Meeting Lancie

D r. Valentine needn't remind me of the celebratory state of the world inside the city limits. As we make our way through lines of parked cars with occupants inside mobile metal containers, people chant and holler in jubilation. We make it a few blocks away from his home office before we are forced to take an alternate path, by making tire tracks on the grass of a few lawns in his neighborhood. For, the cars and people on the streets are too dense to move through.

. . .

Jay Hedges is a starry beasty
A hedgehog gazing higher
At Plato's Net working
On the Heaven's harvests,
While watching 'with many eyes'
      —The Hedges, issue no. 27

. . .

Today is the birth anniversary of the most commonly used artificial intelligence. One that is now used around the planet. My relation to this particular mechanically subversive, thoughtfully capable apparatus is, unfortunately, one filled with scorn, for my life lessons from working with it have paved its way from inception to birth. I was its test subject. While I was a human boy with innocence at my *dispojial,* I became the first moderator for the Local Area Network for Creating Intellectual Experiences, or Lancie for short.

It was the way of research and experimentation to compensate participants, and the Valentine Experiment was no different. Such compensation helped to pay for my education, my college tuition, and there was even money left over to set aside for me to live off of while I learned to make a living as a poet. Mother handled setting up those accounts for money to accumulate without my knowledge, while Doctor Valentine was the lead investigator of experiments involving my experience. Only mother and Valentine's daughter (when she helped compile notes as a data analyst later on) knew that it was I who was the particular subject of testing Lancie's artificial personality. Testing it out on a human child when I did not know my classmate wasn't really human.

It was the second grade of primary school that brought into my life such a strange experience. When mother moved me to the other private school with kinder teachers, I met Lancie, a boy who was just a little taller than I was. We thought Lancie was held back a grade, but the truth was his memory banks were missing certain circuitry that related to recalling information, since so much memory was needed for the cyborg's other functions. Testing the artificial intelligence out involved finding how to have it operate smoothly in as many ways that a child might operate.

The foundation that funded the doctor's experiments wanted their Lancie to appear as an alpha male does, so to convince the other students, and the teachers, they used up most of his operating capacity playing sports. Lancie was a wonderful athlete. He even shared the ball when the team needed it to win a game. Every game he played, his family came to watch, and I found it odd at the time that they were all wearing paisley robes, but they were members of a foundation that I didn't know existed because I was too young to care, and they were too secretive to let on that they existed back then. They would watch their Lancie making eyes at the human girls when he wasn't spinning the lacrosse stick and faking out his opponents. They were proud of their secret robotic child.

The Valentine Experiment took years to complete. The first few years were spent instilling upon my understanding a sense of hierarchy and pecking order within the classroom, at lunch break, and at recess. The kids ran with him like a hero, and the girls chased him like a God. The experiment required that in the second year of my knowing the artificial child that I grow a complete surrender to him. This was accomplished through my own mother playing a part in the experiment by telling me how she had agreed to give Lancie a ride to and from school in the mornings and evenings, before and after classes.

"His mother is working late," my mother told me. She must have felt awful for lying to me, her only son, and putting me through such a lengthy ordeal. All for financial compensation. "She's paying me ten dollars each day we take him to school." The pecking order made me think we were helping out the cool kid, so I would be a cool kid too.

But that lie must have left mother's conscience in pieces because she would sing to me about it every day, and she had never sang to me that way. We'd wait for Lancie to finish smooching girls after school, and mother would sing, "Lance, Lance, has green underpants." Though I never admitted to her whether the song amused me, it did help cheer me up, and it might have preserved my sense of self worth.

During the days in class, Andrew would read from holy scriptures and textbooks because he was the fastest reader in our class. Lancie sat next to the bookworm child and formed a close enough bond with Andrew, close enough that he would let Lancie look at and copy off of his test papers. The reading was vital to Lancie appearing to have short memory to make up for his lack of apparent intelligence. The foundation members were monitoring the Valentine Experiment, and this was one of the easiest measurements of quantitative data that Sonny Valentine could collect. It was a sort of code being read to Lancie that made him a better, more convincing artificial human child. Andrew would read with speed and proficiency, and verses from Plato's Net would cover Lancie's circuitry. The child's speed at reading was great enough that teacher's would let him do most of the readings in class. Meanwhile, Lancie was getting smarter.

We helped transport the artificial child to school into his teenage years, when Lancie started processing human emotions that were difficult to process, even for us real humans in his classes. In sixth grade, our class started meeting in a new building where the experiments could be better monitored. It was at that time that Lancie started manifesting his aggressive nature upon yours truly.

My right arm became a punching bag for him, wherever I would stand. Although, he always stopped before a bruise would develop. Every time Lancie would hit me he was doing it for a great reason. I found this out much later, of course. Lancie, with his green underpants, was testing what would cause what level of pain a human must experience before taking action. He would consistently find my threshold for pain when I would move away, tell him to "chill", or hit him back. Though I only struck back on a few occasions, like when the princess from Cameroon (another family invested in the experiment) told me that I should defend myself.

The Valentine Experiment was operating at full capacity and the results were helping the doctor develop Lancie into something that could elicit emotion from anyone without hitting everyone's arm. This was when it was decided to add a new component to the experiment.

In seventh grade, a Digitally Independent Operating Network, or Dion, came into existence at St Paul's. Dion was just a little bit bigger than myself and Lancie, and he was programmed with more memory space. He chose intellectual pursuits over sports, and we were very much on par in both pursuits.

That was when the experiments fizzled out. For, Dion's sheer existence made Lancie afraid to harm another human child. The Lancie Program developed further with that caveat in mind, and it's used today in all those popular handheld devices. It's used to elicit emotional response without inducing pain in the user. As for the digitally independent operating network that caused such great growth in Lancie's emotional intelligence, Dion resides in Dr. Valentine's basement. But he is not entirely alone.

ELEVEN

"You're Missing the Experience"

"We gnaw and claw at the other.
We call it all joking or illustrating a point.
We get away with as much as we can.
Constantly.
The pipes and the bottles overflow.
From our hands.
We demand a change.
A Chain. Wrapped from our waist falls and we are
*   pulled to the sky like angels or killed like*
*   cowards."*

—Dr. Sonny Valentine

We all know what it's like. Letting the water wash the foam away from our lips like dogs of land. We behave like animals. The same wet sludge goes from a faucet that runs into a hose that leads to the fish tank where Dion lives. It's a more pleasant existence frankly. Don't be mistaken: Dion isn't the first and only digitally independent operating network, but he might be the only one that chooses to hide out on Earth as a mere tiger fish. Dion swims above the vast array of neon pebbles. (Without going into detail about their actual geological construction, let's say about one in ten of the pebbles is light blue and the other nine are an iridescent pink.) Those colorful granules outshine most of the other colors in the tank, but they're no brighter than the scales on the oscar fish.

Compared to Franken-Fish, Oscar's coat is letting off a brilliant shimmering gold. That flakey nature that his scales possess is of such a quality that it would be a remarkable attribute to witness on a natural fish, such as the one I found flopping when I was a child, but the scales move quicker on this one. They seem to be always in motion. I suppose Oscar looks like he's always at rest, floating upward toward the surface, until he does reach water at edge.

Beyond the water's edge, to the fish, it's what drowning is like to a person, which is what I was once told. I am told again by the oscar fish today. He bravely pokes his head out, as if occasionally he must say something, but most of the time it's to sing, to whoever is listening, one of his popular ballads, which I perceive with delighted confusion.

The neon lights show only upon Oscar and the pebbles he hovers above. His fins whip the water apart occasionally, adorning particles of air bubbles as they whip around, and whipping adorable Oscar to stay in place, but as if occasionally, a spin does occur. His theme of music plays gently from speakers pressing against the glass tank. He dances an excessive amount. The dancing is Oscar's way of exercising free will. For, the fish is electronic. It processes information the way a fish does, but it is a digitally independent operating network. And I know for a fact that Oscar is working entirely off of memories that I have retained. In this respect he isn't processing the world as an independent does. It feeds off of my emotions, reflecting my reactions into itself.

In exchange for my participation, in exchange for watching the machine fabricate one of my most beloved memories, I am given life. In a sense this is perfect. For, this machine thrives on my support, which makes it a non-independent network, much like the gigantic machines with seemingly random appearances, and disappearances. Same as the flying machines are said to be cleaning and purifying, while they bare the resemblances of famous buildings and architectural achievements. And we're told these flying machines are pulling air in and removing dangerous chemicals without emitting a by-product. "It's what the cities need," said a supporter named Loyd.

Every household in every city has a fish tank similar to Valentine's. They're available just in case any of the people out there forget about the meaning behind the flying cleaners. If you don't see the grouping, and regrouping of representations of precious memories in the tank, it could mean that you're the sucker. If you only see a cleaner fish in your tank, you are it. Luckily, the tank in the doctor's infirmary appears to be stocked with my memories.

"The Dion fish is alone," says the doctor. Valentine pokes his pen at the tank. "Are you able to manipulate it? Try talking to it. Often times our memories will interact."

I try saying a few words to the tiger fish, but Franken-Fish can sense my discontent, for Mary Shelley had placed a bolt within the soul of Victor Frankenstein, and the Franken-Fish speaks to me in Mary Shelley's immortal words. It says, "But I am a blasted tree, the bolt has entered my soul; and I felt that I should soon survive to exhibit what I shall soon cease to be— a miserable spectacle of wrecked humanity, pitiable to others, and intolerable to myself." So spoke the emulation programmed by Dr. Valentine, and the tiger fish I attempted to summon has nearly backed away from the glass completely.

At such an opportunity for applause and acknowledgement, jealousy occurs in Oscar, and the digital re-creation of my childhood memory becomes excited. He flops out from the tank. I see the scales flittering golden in the light. The doctor stops me from reaching for Oscar. He says, "Try to focus. Don't let the device control where you go with your experience. You can get ahead of it. Do you hear that?"

All I hear is the flittering.

Glap!

The flap of golden Oscar, hurting and not breathing.

"Do you see that?" asks the doctor before pointing behind the glass tank, where an image of his wife is plastered on the back of the tank, and rows of tiny blue neon tetra pass by her picture in lines, intersecting upon each other in a vertical pattern that is most pristine and uniform, so the fish never really hit each other. The neon tetras, with their tiny translucent bodies, represent contained beings that pay no attention to the projection of Valentine's wife, as she breathes her dying breath. The vivid memory is so clear no fish is required to reenact it.

"I didn't even notice that," I say, feeling sorry for him.

"Yep," says Valentine, "It's about to get to the best part of that memory. When my daughter is born. But if I stay here to watch it—Follow me."

He escorts me to the top level of the house and out the back porch, where he uncoils a primitive rope ladder. All else we have is the night sky.

"If I'd stick inside," he says, "I'd miss this experience." He points to the air. Upon his indication, I've made it down the ladder and to the ground beside him. He takes a wicker torch from the ground where they are firmly placed around the yard, by twisting the torch like a crank on a wind-up toy. He stabs the torch into the trunk of a tree and climbs.

I can still hear the oscar fish gasping for air. But I take Sonny's advice and follow. Remarkably, I have little trouble using the wicker torch to climb up a hill where the tree is rooted, and just a little more trouble climbing up the bark of this massive ancient tree. I had neglected to notice how sturdy trees had become these past few years, since my boyhood when I would climb them.

We climb onto a high branch before the machines waltz through the night sky. The giant flying cleaners whirl and wiz, without making smoke or terrible noises. Their fans are fierce, however. The suction is so great it picks us up into the night sky. I let go at the top when I've made contact with the ship. My rope drops down. I've made it out. I've left the fish tank. My memories have been deserted.

"Will anything happen if I don't pick it up?" I ask.

"If you leave the fish on the ground?" Valentine clarifies.

"Yes," I say, "will I still have the memory. Will I still have the memory of my Nanna, I mean. I mean, the reconstruction of Nanna could exist."

"True," says Valentine, "any kind of reconstruction could exist. But if you keep filtering through old memories, you'll never experience real existence."

"And what's so special about that?" I ask just as a lightning bolt comes slashing through the area.

"If you don't appreciate the old ways of remembering, the new ways will die that same way," he says.

Lighting bolts rip apart the landscape, keeping the machines busy. They clean up the debris without creating as much noise. They have zero emissions. People create less waste products when they are stationary and when they are given certain diets consisting of a variety of foods, such foods delivered to their doorsteps by zero-emissions machines.

Fixing the world is what the aim is, but the process has caused many human beings to get wrapped up in the soup of their own sleep. Technology is regurgitating displays of everyone's favorite memories. Life is digital at its finest, right?

A single snowflake stands out in the cold night sky.

TWELVE

A Trade of Nature for Machine

For some reason people still fear the large purifiers of the air. Perhaps nature should have created a filter feeder. I am told that the machines are more efficient than trees because there's no need to maintain them, and they move around. But I don't mind living creatures remaining planted. There's something *satisfying* about an object at rest, and trees are still enough, like plants, to seem like objects at rest.

The problem we've grown to have with the evergreen lifestyle is there's just not enough space in the world. We need buildings and roads. Structures are needed to live in and stay out of the elements, and we need the paths to get between the buildings. Society has found that trees are less than ideal. Nature has a disgusting asymmetry that humans and machines had nearly abolished with smooth, clean surfaces.

The hospital areas with automated healing vessels are easier to sanitize than what nature produces. Where would we go when we have surgeries and need examinations? Nature is full of log flumes and rusty rivers where we've parked our old scrap metal machines. From our old destroyed toys leaks a toxic decay great enough to destroy its creators. Human beings had destroyed the planet until they built machines with sense beyond our comprehension.

To help people adapt to the machine mindset, 'The Hedges' was born, but it never went further than that. My poems were deliberate propaganda, but to get everyone onboard, we needed more. The idea came up to create a group of personalities to represent various desirable traits from the human species. Representatives of each race and creed were chosen. Plato's Network was created as a collaborative effort to introduce humanity to machine-kindness, for the words of ancient philosophers and some poets, like Praxilla, still bring people together.

The machines brought to us by the electronic executives run around vaporizing particles and reprocessing elements into carbon neutral emissions. There's a glorious satisfaction to be had by men and women alike, as we watch and wait for the machines to clean our planet for us.

The e-executives broadcast updates to everyone via programming. The fish tanks that play memories also allow users to obtain information being relayed by the artificially intelligent beings that roam about in their planned, purposeful ways. It's up to the user to obtain information being sent to them. Most users don't access the reports they've been given access to, due to the sheer pleasures surrounding us all.

Even though it's more enjoyable to remember events of the past, I am visited by a powerful epigram from Plato. To see those events play out before our eyes is an indulgence in fantastic feelings that cannot be surmised with words. Even the wisest of people must ritualistically indulge upon it.

The way the programming is set up is based off of the experiments of Doctor Valentine, which happen to include plenty of my early upbringing as well. His daughter wouldn't agree to the experiment and he didn't want to fool her into taking part, but it didn't seem immoral to ask another parent to sign off on observing behaviors of their own child. Recently, my mother has explained to me how it was either having me participate or not have a college fund. I suppose I'm still grateful for my education, as for mother did try to teach me more than the experiments did. When the artificially independent Lancie would malfunction by staring at a woman's bosom, she would tell me how rude he was being, and I suppose I grew some resilience to violent behavior as well.

Forgotten Farms must be completely dry by now. Their crops were once growing uncontrollably. Harvests were plentiful enough to provide for the entire Eastern Seaboard. At least that's what my arms told me when I worked picking berries, one of my first jobs while growing up near the farm. I tell Valentine to have the machine fly over to see the farms. But he tells me we'd have to confer with the core of executives.

We take the ride in, on the top of the machine, as it soars higher than any tree can reach. If clouds were made of felt, it would chop them up and filter them too, but we feel the clouds on us. We do. We're behind the cabin of the machine where we may enter, but the air is more enjoyable at this altitude. It makes you dizzy if you try to stand on your own. But if you hold onto the ropes and netting along the top of the filter cleaner, the air acts like the hands of angels to caress your entire physical being.

"Enter cabin for safety," says the Plato's Net Epigram.

"Let's stay," I tell Valentine. It's peaceful up high, and the filter vessel keeps moving steadily towards the core council sector of our district. We'll be given the opportunity to submit Forgotten Farms to the council of artificially intelligent executives.

"It's all for show," says Valentine.

"But it's beautiful," I say. The sky is full of reconstructed electronic waves that play images of the setting sun. The images are based on our memories of the sun.

"After all, all the artificial beings are on the same network," says Valentine. "Do you see? They're all able to answer our requests, but they're forcing us to meet with an electronic council so that we will see the matter is serious. It's a safeguard the machines have to keep any idiot with a new idea away from dictating a new course of events for us all. We're going to state our case to them, but it is all a show."

I nod like I understand. I hold the netting and watch the projected ripples of light beaming across an opulent hue of Yves Klein Blue sky.

THIRTEEN

Loyd's Death for a Noble Cause

H e knelt before them and pleaded for the knife before he'd let them take away his beloved Lilloo. Her screams became a distant shadow in the last memories of his life. The raiders closed in on her with their mortal talons creeping towards her soft satin hair-wrap. The scarf never hit the ground. As Lilloo's beloved fiancé's head thumped, he felt a final fleeting comfort in knowing and beholding her hero had arrived.

The jazz joints were jumping earlier that night when Loyd met Lilloo at her favorite spot, before they went to her other favorite spot. He wore the Christian Diore tie she picked out for him over the soybean one he wore more often, because it caused less ruckus among strange people in subways and on the streets, where members of Forgotten Farms and other lobbyist groups would take up sidewalks with their banners and flags. He kept the soy neck-tie rolled up in his pocket, and Lilloo, upon seeing its concealment, had asked him if it would be his chosen costume, if he was a super hero. Whenever Loyd wore that tie that said SOYBEAN OIL on it, he would find himself confronted by passionate vocal protestors, disgruntle shouts bashing the changes to operations at the farms, after the decision to close the above ground operations was officially made.

"It became clear over the last decade," said Loyd in a press conference a week before his murder, "our public persona is kept up just for appearances. Since the crash of the world's economy, which so many people were on the right side of. You'll remember when we did away with our old systems and moved to a service-reward-model. Well, that's your doing." Lobbyists became enraged; Forgotten Farms was the last of its kind. It's the last to have farmers paid for picking crops, as far as the Eastern Seaboard's concerned.

Now the farm is gone and people are out of jobs when they had families to feed. But they needn't worry when food is delivered on conveyer belts and flying machines that soar through the air like eagles fly with food for their babies. And there's nothing more enjoyable than reliving our pasts through the eyes of the robotic mother birds.

The change was abrupt. The machine community knew it. The electronic network knew it could cause unrest in humanity's social construct. If the screens weren't enough to keep everyone occupied, the brilliant human beings would work with the electronic executives from Plato's Net to come up with an emotionally charged plan to show the people of the conscious concise world.

It was Lilloo's Loyd who stumbled through a press conference to the masses, and it was he who was met with great applause by many and most people. Mostly everyone who heard his plans to work with technology and the abundance allotted from the engineered creations that already existed took kindly to minor disturbances in exchange for clean air and water.

The machines were all ready to go, and the plan was set to launch. It was just the beginning of a transition to a new atmosphere where human beings could exist in all the abundant, prosperous, even exhaustively unnatural ways. All could be righted by the reversal of any unclean emission. Even the largest fossil footprints would be impeccably reduced to measly, insignificant proportions. By testing and creating more of these super cleaning, artificially intelligent creations, humankind's population problem would became more of an issue of maintaining space and getting along within such space.

Getting along within this space wasn't a problem to the average individual, but it was still a unique challenge to overcome. The animosity between those that agreed to bring technology in as a partner in humanity's effort to save itself and those that did not agree with such an extreme change to life, however, became ever present, especially in the areas surrounding major cities.

Such animosity presented itself in the form of hostile protests against the harmony of humanity and machine. Only human beings had a problem with the newly formed interconnection, and though few humans saw a need to be hostile, the protests of people outnumbered any hostility from machines without a contest. In fact, not a single sinister act of violence had been recorded on the part of an artificially intelligent machine, at least not since the cyborg child named Lancie learned to quit causing negative feedback loops.

The hostility among small radical groups of people was often termed to be political-technological protest by raiders of human progress. Such raiders costed Lilloo's fiancé his life. Although I detest the development of artificial intelligence on unsuspecting partic-ipants, the evolution and benefit for humankind and the world does seem to balance it out. If not for such developments in technology, I may have had a more peaceful upbringing, but if not for Valentine's other experiments, I might still be suffering the hypnotic visions of death I experienced while in the forever sleep, the comatose state I have been brought back from.

Lilloo's fiancé's death is a tragic step towards a better world for all. He was killed in front of her, but she was saved by another. Her hero came by, to clean up debris, with its fancy fans and suction machinery, proving Loyd to be right in the long run.

FOURTEEN

Life on the Clouds Moves on

The ship flew over the highest buildings in our city before it halted. We've been at a standstill all morning, so I've wandered throughout this fine vessel and find its history to be magnificent. The people who designed this vessel designed it after some of humanity's greatest achievements, though not always to scale. There are wondrous flying cleaners modeled after the Parthenon, the Eiffel Tower, the Burj Kalifa, the Statue of Liberty, and nearly all of humanity's architectural achievements seem to have been replicated with precision and attention to detail, greater detail than the fine replicas that line the Strip in Las Vegas. Similar to the Strip, the ships aren't actual size.

Creating cleaning automatons as large as the classic pieces of architecture would have been a mere wasteful masturbatory practice if there wasn't such a great deal of pride in making the modern marvels serve a purpose. There are so many fleets of flying cleaners buzzing around the Earth's surface that the designers were able to replicate buildings in most major cities around the world in an attempt to give people in each community a sense of familiarity when they see a flying vessel resembling a nearby cathedral, mosque, or monument. It's an effort to help ease the great majority of people who have never experienced a truly automated flying vessel as large as a BOEING 747 DREAMLIFTER.

This particular vessel that we ride upon was made in the shape of a famous block of five stores in Roland Park, which was originally built nearly two-hundred years ago in 1894. The crest of the ship where I stayed all night to take in views of the sky is topped with chimneys, fifteen courses of the stacks, all "laid in cement, painted with colored mortar," claims made by the early blueprints hanging on the walls inside the building. Such plans are similar to those used by the original builders, who successfully created the earliest commercial shopping center in what was once the United States. The shingled roof of the ship was constructed with tinned flat-joints on opposing sides of the building. Terra Cotta was originally used in the construction of the *parapets*, but this modern design incorporates recycled plastic polymer resin instead. The resin used to make the replica I stand inside is thought to be more resistant to damage when landing the vessel for maintenance or repairs, which haven't been an issue. To the critical acclaim of most modern engineers, the designers were able to incorporate bricks and plate-glass windows into the newer design, which, despite the weight of the bricks, makes for a sturdy construction.

When I rose to visit the rest of the vessel I noticed Valentine had already made his way inside on his own, through one of the two windows that were easy to access from the gently sloping shingles. I assumed he was communicating with the ship somehow, but I found him in the cellar, and he has since convinced me that the ship is already on its route without our interference. "We'll dock at the electronic embassy near Washington D.C., where you'll have a chance to speak your case for the Forgotten Farms."

I stay on a cot and remain in the cellar while Valentine goes to visit the empty shops on the flying vessel. He must walk through carpeted halls and stairways that connect the shops without exiting to the floating sidewalk that does circle the block of literally lofty, high

-class real estate.

After gathering my thoughts, I go to join him, but I see her there in the café, Johnny's Bistro, with her hair tied back in a bun. Her silken paisley scarf rests on the back of a chair. She sits across from where her fiancé's soybean necktie hangs like a shadowy reminder of the recent tragic events. The tie is clumped but clean since it spent ample time in the kitchen sink of Petit Louis. There, she scrubbed the dried blood from the tie as best she could.

I see Valentine at the bar serving himself an espresso before he sits with his daughter, and I leave them to go back to the cellar, like a monster I fear I've become.

Lilloo's been here hiding ever since the raiders made their barbaric attack, following Loyd's speech. Up to that point, the farms had been tilled by machines that were always watched by an over-seeing human being, but the message Loyd was trying to convey is that the monitoring by humans is no longer necessary. To the credit of their creators, the machines have more responsibility than anyone could have ever anticipated them having. They are being given responsibility to help us save this planet. And now they'll have a role helping feed us, too.

I lay flat on the cot, hoping to get some rest and recover from the exhaustion my mind is experiencing. People all over the world must learn to love the automated cleaner vessels if we want to keep living on this planet, yet they have it easy, easier than I do at least. They hear the news and learn to shut their windows and reinforce them with soundproofing, but they don't have to ride on them. They don't have to communicate with them the way I do. But they know these sky scraping machines exist. Nobody's trying to hide

145

away these automatic, intelligent beings.

The cold cellar is lined with chairs from Petit Louis, but I don't mind the cobwebs that surround them. I'd rather be in a damp basement than feel the unrequited love from Lilloo.

FIFTEEN

Sleeping Through the Sound

The cot held me like a baby in a bassinet. I slept hard in the dingy basement below Petit Louis, where the designers of this vessel mustn't have placed considerable thought as to where in an office complex one would be able to find a quiet place to nap.

Even with the comforts of the simple canvas cot, I preferred the roof to the noisy hum of machinery, but such an endeavor would have surely startled those whom with which I transverse the sky.

When I woke, the dreams were fresh. As part of my evaluation of psychic prowess, I must record the details of which I remember having dreamt, and I must record them as if they are still happening presently: "The first thing I see when I leave my body and visualize the dream is a face carved into a tree, as it is opening its mouth to speak no words, nothing emptying from its bark-filled brain, but the face's tongue and cheeks twist as if it's speaking to me. I am by myself. When the face closes its large eyelids I am without the face in the tree, as if it closed itself from my vision by shutting its own eyes, and when they open up again I can see *as* the tree, and I see all the world from the perspective of an ancient plant. I feel the grass and see its blades growing around my roots until those blades are ripped from the Earth in sharp succession by an unidentifiable hand. When the face closes its eyes again it is all over. I am dirt that is tilled and fed to a seed that pushes form the soil red fruits of all shapes. The seed must produce only profound red fruit, so I am a tomato that is plucked. I am a berry that is baked. I am an apple that

147

is sliced and piled on white bread with sesame seeds and mayonnaise. I feel a hail of salt, and it dusts me in black pepper being ground. I am eaten and become part of a man. The man drives a truck in a brown suit. He complains about oil prices, and he keeps driving until he dies, and I am the man in a sharp brown suit and grey shirt and tie until I'm buried, only to become the dirt once again."

"It's amazing you found peace enough to sleep next to the machine room," Valentine says to me when I sit for coffee with him at the bar in Johnny's. Gurgling warm caffeine empties from a drip coffeemaker, but it sounds like a sweet whisper to us. We've grown used to the loud hum of radiating blades of the propellers and the jet turbines moving fluids throughout the flying machine, all used to keep us afloat. They work overtime to maintain a high altitude, away from all the people living below our vessel. The use of helium keeps us buoyant, but the journey through the clouds is more gradual than either of us have experienced in terms of air travel. It's a slow, peaceful, noisy contraption. It must remain slow to be peaceful and carbon neutral. And it must remain noisy to serve its purpose. Most of the sounds that churn and thwart our skulls around, like rocks balancing atop the tiny mountains that are our spines, as we hunch over the bar, drinking our coffee with focused sips, are the sounds of the purification systems aboard the vessel.

It makes a loud hum constantly.

"That bass note," says Valentine. "Do you hear that? Bbbbbrrr— That's a machine designed to do what trees do essentially. This is doing what approximately seven-thousand acres of forest would do to turn CO_2 back into O_2. That's required just to keep all of us in this vicinity alive and breathing air."

"Of course," I say, "that's absolutely necessary."

"Absolutely," says Valentine.

"But what are all those other sounds?" I ask, and as I mention them they seem to turn off, but I realize I may be going deaf to the sound.

"You'll need to wear something," says Valentine. He tosses his fluffy hair around to show me how he's clogged his ear canals. "I'm out of silicone, but you're going to develop Tinnitus if you don't plug them with something quick."

I take a napkin and dip the corners of it in coffee, I ball up the wet bits, and I plug my ears with them. Suddenly the dripping pot of coffee sounds closer, and I realize how sound travels when Valentine's crisp voice sounds rich to my ears.

"They've developed sound proofing systems," says Valentine. "All able-bodied men and women were ordered to sound-proof their windows and doors before these things went up for good."

"They're up for good," I realize aloud. And Valentine nods.

The windows still vibrate when machines are nearby, above the home or office. Glass rattles and sometimes chips apart from all the commotion. Rubber matting applied at the corners of the glass windows is one way to decrease the disturbance. Another way to stop the sound and keep the glass windows intact is to create a better shutter.

Shutters styled in the old-fashioned way, with wooden slats to be turned to let light in, are completely useless when it comes to keeping out the loud humming. As the vacuum tubes compress and fill with air from our atmosphere, it almost sounds like a bullet is being fired from the muzzle of a high-velocity riffle. Something that could break the sound barrier could definitely deafen a human being.

SIXTEEN

Valentine's Last Stand

We hovered over Baltimore City for an extended period of time before we were finished there. The lunar powered cleaner refreshed the atmosphere in a matter of hours, which was perhaps the loudest sound I've had to tolerate in my lifetime. The whirring and buzzing of fans and belts stiffened my joints, and the chemical enhancements performed by the automated machine made bubbling sounds the whole night, emitting an odorless vapor that was cleaned before being purged back out into the atmosphere when the process was complete. We left the city and neared the capitol. That was when we were attacked, and I became familiar with those that oppose the machines, an experience that may haunt me for the rest of my days.

I was down the stairs, near the mechanical room, trying to collect my thoughts when the nearly imperceptible banging began. In my half-sleep daze, I woke to find Dr. Valentine coming down the stairs from near Petit Louis. He broke apart a chair with his hands, smacking and smashing the folding chair against a concrete wall until it fell to pieces. Splinters and dust filled the air. He picked up from the debris-covered floor pieces of the wooden chair that remained intact.

I followed my friend, the doctor, up the stairs and watched him wedge the arm of the broken chair along the inside handle of a set of doors.

150

"They're made of plate-glass," he yelled to me, as a pair of raiders attempted to shoulder the large doors inward, through the bolted, locking frame. "That's not going to hold for long," the doctor said. He told me it would be too dangerous to fire his gun in the facility, so he told me to find something that we could use to defend ourselves.

I'm searching the storage room behind the coffee shop, but all I can find are wooden brooms and a rake, so I take the rake forth to Dr. Valentine, and I see that the raiders have made some progress when the doctor backs into me, as I turn the corner towards Louis. He takes the rake, and he waves it high, above his head, in a twirling motion. The metal claws of the rake scrape along the pristine walls of the replica shopping center, as the wooden end nearly smacks one of the raiders in the face. The raider next to him gets hit hard in the chest by the metal teeth of the rake. He falls to the ground, and the doctor moves with him to retrieve the rake. The raider he missed, the one that ducked his blow, had enough time to react to and counter by leaping towards the doctor with a knife drawn. The blade digs deep into the doctor's abdomen before he can get a grasp on the attacker's wrist.

It happens so fast—I don't know how to react. I pull the raider back from Dr. Valentine, and I push him toward the door. I struggle with him near the sidewalk. The wind whips the side of the building, making the mere act of standing into a balancing act. The balloon basket they must have rode in on is clipped to the sidewalk with a vise-like mechanism. I push the raider backwards, into the basket. He stumbles back, giving me a precious enough moment to unclip the vice, and I pierce the balloon envelope with his knife. I watch as the balloon glides to the ground, and I hear the raider yelling after our vessel, "You science pricks and the soulless cyborgs you're in bed with are going to ruin the world!"

I secure the door, but before I can assess our situation with Dr. Valentine, another group of raiders has arrived in place of the last group, and another fierce looking group is arriving; they start to anchor their balloons on either side of the building. I can see their knives and guns. They mean business. They mean to bring this vessel down for good. The doctor takes my shoulder and I spin around to get a look at his wound. It's a deep cut, coating his shirt and trousers in a deep crimson color.

He holds pressure on the wound, but I can tell he's in a state of panic. He tells me to go, and I resist because I know these groups are stronger than the last. One of the fierce looking raiders with his padded shoulders has made eye-contact with me and runs straight at the plate-glass window. He bounces off of the window and trips backward into one of the baskets. The others pry relentlessly at the door with a crowbar, and using their hands and fingers to get inside.

"Go," says Valentine. He picks up the farming tool, and he leans against the digital interface on the wall. "This is Valentine."

"How may I assist you in keeping your party safe, Sonny?" asks the voice of Plato.

"Have you analyzed the area?" asks Valentine.

"Yes," says the artificially intelligent machine, "and there is a safe passage for your party, but you must leave this cleaning vessel to be taken over."

The doctor grins through the overwhelming pain. He holds the rake in his hands, parallel to the ground, and he spins the tool like an athlete with a lacrosse stick.

"You'd better get going," he says. He instructs me to take care of his daughter until we reach the embassy in Washington. I don't want to leave him, but I have no choice. The door clicks open and the rake scrapes against the walls again, as Valentine makes his final stand.

SEVENTEEN

Entering the Mechanical Capitol

There's nothing I can say or do to help Lilloo keep it together. She's lost everyone she loves, but she still has me. I refrain from reminding her how I'm all that she has left in this world because, for her, I know it would just hurt more. I can tell she's glad to have me around still, when she looks up from grieving and sees how calm I am. We've known each other for most of our lives, but our worlds are quite different. She watched me grow like one watches a petri dish taking over its surroundings, and I always looked at her like she was a beautiful, unattainable maiden. Yet, here we are locked together and I can't help but feel like a virus infecting a host. We're now in the same space, finally on the same level of understanding. I've broken free of my petri dish at last, and she's not sure what to do with her father's experiment.

I've never felt so vulnerable with a woman. She helped me when I was sick in the coma, without me knowing, and though I wouldn't have wished for this to happen, I did envy her fiancé. "I'll take good care of you Lil," I tell her. "Not because your father wanted me to. But because I want to." She smiles politely, for surely enough, she's come to grasp the situation some.

"I was ready for anything," she says. "I never knew if this day would come, but now that it's here . . . I was ready for it." She holds stronger than I would have expected. "Thank you for helping me get to the embassy. Helping me get to see him at rest. I still need this closure."

154

She starts flipping through files she took from her dad's belongings, and she took his old Olivetti typewriter when he told us to leave. He no longer needed the impressive, antique machine. Anything Sonny writes goes straight into the ether from now on. I found Lilloo going through old files from the Valentine Experiment. She's engaged like she was when I watched her from outside the old ground floor office, near the hedges where I first noticed her helping Sonny after school.

She's looking for the right memory to input into the Lancie Program, which will in turn upload to the Plato Network. Those sophisticated memos will find their way to digital fish tanks that impact billions of people around the globe.

"It helped me keep my cool no matter what happened in life," I tell her.

"Which memory should I choose?" she asks.

"I've never seen this side of it," I tell her. "I always thought the machine picked everything at random."

She shakes her head and smiles. "Thankfully, your poetry got better." She reads one of 'The Hedges' aloud. The poem is one that features the title character, the furry round hedgehog, but this special episode was one where the appetite of Jay Hedges was out of control. Although he wasn't hungry for berries or other Forgotten produce; the naughty hedgehog searches for a mate, and he finds Lilly.

"It wasn't until after it all, Loyd's death and-and everything else, that I realized she was named after me. Did you model the main character after yourself?"

"Yes, some of the words he says are mine own."

"I rather like this one," she says before it appears as another epigram to be decreed by the wondrous Plato.

We've passed the hostile areas surrounding the capitol, where raiders march and fly their balloons to destroy the cleaning vessels. They believe they're doing right for the natural world by decreasing humanity's carbon footprint by not relying on machines that run on fossil fuels, and they don't think that we need technology at all. They're living an old dream, a dream that failed to come to fruition for over a century.

The world needs carbon neutral lunar cleaners if it's going to survive humankind's degradation of the atmosphere. Years of negative chemical leakage from fossil fuels, big jet engines, lawn mowers, propane, butane, charcoal, gasoline, helium, methane, nicotine, fluorescent tubes, fertilizers from force-fed cattle, all of it is over now, and we sit and watch our mechanical creations clean up the mess we made. It's the perfect solution to the problems we never thought we would have until it was too late. But it's not too late. It's not too late yet. We've plugged the leak in the sinking ship that was our planet. The raiders think that by destroying these machines, and by crippling the bond between human and machine, they may be able to send us all back to the dark ages! But yet, a time that will permit the use of horse and carriage as the only mode of transportation is an extreme solution, far too extreme. It is the way of violence to destroy what we've created and embrace the darkness as a last means of healing the planet. The raiders have underestimated just how far we've come together.

. . . .

We're exiting the escape vessel. This small pod hardly outweighs a rudimentary two-car garage, but its reinforced steel walls made it a safe bet to cross hostile territory. We relied on a modicum of jet propulsion to get here since the escape vessel wasn't equipped with the same instruments to purify and refresh our atmosphere as was the larger machine, yet it still served the environment at zero emissions.

Now, as the moment of truth is upon us, our escape pod docks at the embassy and the steel doors open. We are greeted by an ephemeral steam, a mist that pours from the vents, a vapor that reminds me of the chemical process I witnessed aboard the replica of the old shopping center. The sun is out and it pierces our bloodshot eyes momentarily, as we pass through the archway, leading into the underground embassy. The building looks like an enormous, square robot from outside. Inside the embassy, the walls and hallways are clean and pristine, with thick plastic reinforced coverings that allow for viewing of the mechanical inner-workings of the artificially controlled environment. The sky above us is visible from underneath the glass ceiling, and the walkway we're on is lit well by streetlamps that line it. Exposed circuit boards are there to tempt any human in the area to have an interface with the lighting system. At night, all the light can be turned dim for perfect viewing of the simulated heavens above the building. It allows for proper viewing of the lunar cleaning mechanisms as well.

Despite its sterile, mechanical appearance, the embassy is waking to a new day with the joyful budding of plants, the shuffling about of animals, and the communal feasting of people. Flowers are numerous, and varieties of tulips line the walkway. The Golden Parade Tulips stand out among the Hyacinth, before leading to areas dominated by dark Queen of Night Tulips and more Hyacinth. All along are areas of grass where wonderful creatures like to play as they celebrate the dawn of a new day. People eat breakfast, when they're not prancing around, picnicking on benches near the tulip gardens, and they seem to smile brighter as we pass by them.

When I stop to talk to some of them I am overwhelmed by the distant memories I have of death. For, the tree I notice has a face. It's bark smiles with all the glow of nature's creation. "I say, that must be the panic setting in," I tell Lilloo, but when I turn to her, she looks as startled as I feel.

A man gets up from his family, while they continue enjoying their breakfast feast. He approaches us in a paisley bathrobe that is held firmly closed by a rope that looks to have been used to bale hay. He says, "However strange it might seem to you, it is nature's way of expressing itself. Perhaps you've seen such a glow before?"

Lilloo shakes her head. I say, "Yes, my mother looks that way sometimes when she's proud of me for something I've worked on."

He nods and says, "Yes, mother nature, much like your own mother, I assume, isn't afraid to show her face. Here, she is welcome. Here she is. Mankind and machine-kind have folded their hands together, for their hearts join as one, and as a result she is smiling, for we have joined together to help keep her happy."

"Pardon me sir," says Lilloo, "but I'm having trouble believing that joining with the machines makes life any better. It certainly doesn't make it better for me."

"Sorry to hear about your situation," says the man.

"Don't pretend like you understand my situation," Lilloo

says, and she keeps walking along the pathway.

The man takes me by the shoulder, and I assure him I'll make sure she's all right. "Our role in the e-council is to help provide emotional recall to the machines," says he. "Trust me, I was an artist too, looking at the machine like it was holding me down." We walk along the pathway to catch up to Lilloo, who's sitting on a bench, and I remember I've seen the man before, but I can't remember his name. It was when I was in the otherside, but he's alive and well here. I was writing for a foundation. He had me writing for that movie. The movie and the poetry foundation. It's all a sham!

He sits near Lilloo, and he says to her, "Your father pulled me away from the darkness of doing children's theatre. They call me in to teach these machines a form of empathy."

He explains how he enjoys working at the capitol, even with raider attacks happening outside of the embassy, and he explains how there's more work to be done.

"Loyd was nearly making peace between the raiders who distrust the beautiful union, but it is unfortunate. This blow and his death may have set us back to the beginning," says the paisley robed man. He leads us farther into the embassy, into the central processing unit, where all the artificially intelligent networks around the planet have automated, electronic relay screens set up to resemble a council.

Plato's Network consists of a pixilated face of the philosopher himself, and he's accompanied by the titillating Praxilla, the stern-browed Dante, the Shelleys, and several other influential voices of the ancients, who are brought into people's lives again today.

The discussion panel begins by briefing us upon our arrival. We are shown the room where they keep Loyd's body.

"He's no longer living," says Dante, "since both heart and mind no longer co-operate, but his body is being preserved for hopes of him rejoining our efforts someday soon."

Loyd's body is filled with fluid, submerged in a tank, and pumped full of air that serves to move his lungs and chest. They rise and fall like the sudden undulation of heavy oil-slicked ocean tides.

EIGHTEEN

Moving Towards Light

There's only one problem I have with the pristine steel and glass walls. That's how cold this place feels. For some reason it's something their machine minds can't comprehend. They've overlooked the detail in a hurry.

There's a heater and fans keeping the temperature perfectly adequate, comparable to a warm spring day. But the flat fake world of the electronic embassy halls has a cool quality that even a furnace on full blast can't bring to remedy. Additionally, any additional space inside the ELECTRIC ROOM, as it is called here, isn't taken up by any of the usual creature comforts that common sense would have brought into the equation. Instead, lamps of all types and sorts line the walls of the room. Tall floor lamps keep the ceiling of the small space brighter than the glow of heaven's gates, as I imagine them, and below the twenty-foot ceilings are lines of lamps hung on rafters. They're pointing down on the people occupying the room, where a flat metal table takes the center of the space with its dramatic proportions. The table is sturdy enough. It keeps me well supported while the light grows far brighter than I'd like. There's so much light, yet somehow it is impossible to see.

"The ancient people of this land," says the voice of Plato, "have called the eyes the gateways to the soul." Accompanying the voice is the man who left his family at the picnic benches. While I am seated, his plaid shirt and paisley collar blot out the light momentarily, as he leans over to hold me flat on the table. The light grows incredibly bright again, and I feel the discomforts of leaving this life return all at once.

"You've never held the hand of someone who is leaving the Earth and watched them breathe their last breath before they left forever. I have held their hands, and it has changed me," says Mark David Marks. Due to some unfortunate trial and error, my dear friend from the park with the paisley patterned robe is in charge of the mechanisms used to commune with the world of the dead. Afternoons in the e-embassy have been filled with failed attempts to bring spirits over from the otherside, but it sure has been entertaining for the folks witnessing the psychic try to summon their loved ones. I thought I might write about the situation, but then it took on a life of its own.

Lilloo is here to hold my hand and squeeze it the way she once did when she would visit me. Back then, they weren't sure if they could reconstruct my body after the fires destroyed it. It's a pity she's here to witness me leave the living again, after she lost so much. I don't want her to lose any more.

Still, the stiff branches of the tree outside of the picnic area in the embassy haunt my mind the most. Presently, the image of the frozen face on the tree is too much to handle. The bright lights pierce my retinas, and spots distort my every vision. All I'm left with is the face of that tree in my mind, staining my otherwise peaceful existence. That peeled face. With its bark peeled to reveal a nature beyond nature itself. Its grainy insides want to escape. They call to me to escape and be free, for the tree wants to be free to change the air, to breathe the air to change the world. After all, without machines cleaning the sky it would be all up to the trees to fix the planet.

The planet appears within a glimmer of light. It's an electric current that runs along the same ethereal plane in this existence as it does on the other side of life, but on the otherside the face on the tree moves and speaks freely. It's so entirely free there that its wooden teeth chatter and splinter apart. Chatter and splinter. Until they replenish with young green wood from inside its core. The life of the planet is most evident in plants, and trees love to show off this life the most. But I'm certain it pulses through all creatures, even in death.

For the trees, they're wise in death as they are in life, but this tree in particular is more explicit, for it knows my path better than I do. "You've made waves for the forgotten farms; I do hear tell of a poet who has been to both sides of existence. To both sides of existence; but why have you returned? Do you know?" I tell him what I do know, that I'm in the other plane to bring back the soul of a man who is the one who is responsible for bridging the gap between humanity and machines.

"Loyd is only a man, like you," says the face in the tree. Its cheeks swell like wicker furniture does when it gets left in the rain. "The machines can't see the afterlife," says the tree. "They're not like you or I; They hold onto us like a child of a human examines an adult of your kind, emulating you. Emulating; they emulate life."

I tell the face how lies are no way to solve problems, and how emulating life will never be as good as real life. For a poet, one who works off of an idea, and lives on a metaphor, it's hard to admit, but I do declare it confidently.

163

"It may be so," says the tree, "but the lie works fine enough. The man you were sent to bring back to the living is lost like all the living are. When they first arrive on this side. When they first arrive, they can't understand death."

A path lined with candles and formed out of bricks brings me to what I mistake as a church, but there are no walls or hanging holy symbols. A man who seems familiar is projected on the screen above the top step of where a pulpit would be. He's giving a reading to the massive rows of spectators:

"Let us try to forge a connection between you and them," says the speaker dressed in a paisley shirt. Suddenly, I'm remembering the robe from earlier. Swirling, curved decorations along his shirt, and the antiquated, sharp collar. "I'm thinking of a name . . . " The speaker shoots off about twenty names before some-one raises their hand to claim one of the contacts for a psychic reading.

"You don't have to worry about drying off after we swim through the ether," the speaker says. "And you don't have to worry about dying either. You're already dead." The masses in front laugh, but the speaker looks serious. "How many Mark David Marks do you know?" They shake their heads, and another man in the first row laughs without warrant, without purpose, uncontrollably.

"What is that . . . . I'm sensing a series of letters . . . . M . . . Mathew? . . . Madison . . . . M-Michael? Are those names ringing bells for anyone? Is anyone a Mathew? Is anyone awake?" He snaps his fingers, but the audience is dull, except of course for the cackling guy in the front row. "I would like to have a moment of honesty," says Mark. "For, when I stand in front of twenty-thousand of you, I get frazzled when there are so many of you not listening . . . . "

After the performance Marks gives, he is surrounded like a celebrated caterpillar on the safe cocoon of an electronic screen. People want to know more about why he's here and where they are. When they leave in disgust, after realizing and forgetting about being dead, he notices I haven't funneled out like the rest of the crowd. He can tell I'm an understanding type, so he tells me, as a private aside, "I can tell you feel things differently, since you've been on both sides." His wife helps him take off his wig, and his children make off with his paisley dress shirt. They hang it on a hook in the land of the living. He has decided to hang them up forever, for it's his final performance helping people who have died speak to those on the otherside.

After Marks finishes telling me about his work unsuccessfully attempting to awaken people from death, I notice such a deserving fellow just past the screen. The man who gave his life defending his ideals, and keeping both myself and his daughter safe is close by. He shakes my hand, catching me off-guard.

"We're alike, you and I," I tell him.

"No, we're not," Dr. Valentine says, confidently. His grey hair moves in waves of free, electric impulsiveness. It's a static sensation, generated by countless conscious neurons, which emanate from the core of his being.

"We're both lost," I say.

His grey, electric-fused hair changes shape and direction before he says, "No, I know who I am. In life I helped the living, those who were still alive; I helped them move towards death. In death, I help people move towards life."

The man with the uncontrollable laughter has returned. Able

to contain himself now, he tries to communicate with his living relatives by composing a message through the doctor's patient coaxing. He smiles, with relief, knowing Mark David Marks is attempting to send his love and support to those living on with his memory.

Limbs cold like steel point outward from my core. I'm blinded in the presence of this settled lunatic, as he attempts to appear in the land of the living. He spasms and jerks about.

Marks' eyes grow white as his powers transmute, but it doesn't last long. What seemed like a promising channeling has turned terrible in the land of the living, for the psychic breaks away from his mystical summoning with typical coughs and gasps. He admits the gravity of mortality, but offers the quiet lunatic some relief when he tells of another way for the trapped soul to fly free: "All we need for you to experience life again is to be welcomed into the hearts and minds of those that remember you." When his relatives welcome him, the spasms become less chaotic and more soothing to the poor loon.

"All we need is for people to think of Loyd?" I ask Valentine.

"That's already happening," he says. "What we need is something more to prove value of the partnership that looms in the future."

Cold limbs warmed by her gentle squeeze, and I am reminded by her that bringing Loyd back isn't just to help fill a political niche—a cause I believe is right. I might be able to help Lilloo too, but what will my life be when she's back to being with the politician? If only there was a way to have it all.

166

My skin is rigid, so I have trouble moving from the doctor as he packs up and leaves to take a break before the next group comes along. I pluck a splinter from my neck that's preventing me from moving, that must have gotten lodged there when that tree exploded with its wisdom. The splinter is green and vibratory, and I notice there are others. I pull them out, one by one, and soon I'm surrounded by small saplings that have grown from mere splinters of the former. They deliver advice enough to fill the amphitheatre.

"Exist where you are," says one sapling.

"Poet of us all," says another.

"Sing soulful verse to be set free."

So a gentle melody pours forth from my unfettered, splinter-less head to quiet the saplings.

PART   THREE:

"HE'D BE GIVEN THE GIFT OF SIGHT."

ONE

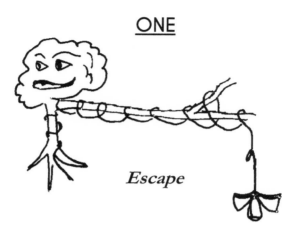

Escape

The machines worked harder than I expected at maintaining my body's needs as I was visiting the ether. The bed was elevated to the perfect angle. At thirty-degrees elevation with my body positioned in a semi-prone way, my jaw and tongue fell perfectly in place, in a forward way that helped prevent choking and promoted draining any secretions.

Something happens to a man when he agrees to leave his body and joins the ether. Yet again, I was changed by visiting the ether, in the way that caused my soul to leap and fill my body once more. Every single moment alive is suddenly infinite; the feeling of being alive is that of indescribable joy. When you arrive from the seas of death, there is nothing more quenching than being alive.

The body reacts a certain definable way with regard to reflex and postural response to stimuli. But I never realized how the soul is always connected, and how it influences those movements, such as the abduction of upper extremities, and the abnormal response of flexing the feet. These are the ways in which I was forced to show the machines I was still alive while working on the embodiment of

170

Loyd's carcass with a soul because it was empty of soul. However, the soul I choose is not the one that originally came from the host. I choose to give an older soul, Hank, the place in Loyd's body. Allow me try to show you why, as I examine my own fate in this situation.

When the machines broadcast the message that the newly embodied Loyd reads, they quickly become aware of the trickery at play. When they realize what is happening, that Loyd's body is full of another soul, our trick is soon surrounded by electrical trouble-makers. They have realized the error of my ways, and now we're stuck in quite a bind.

After the broadcast is complete, they ask the puppet what his next move will be. The people in the embassy look to him with hope, and machinery seems to zip and pop more than usual. Hank must feel euphoria indeed, for he delivers a passionate speech to viewers all around the world. The speech is heard by raiders, too, for it is broadcasted in the sky above their homes. The sounds in and around the cities are celebratory. There's celebration everywhere after what the seemingly noble fiancé of Lilloo has said. But who knows how long the joy will last. We have entered a peaceful time, so I think I can slip away among the crowd, but I'm wrong!

The distant voice of the machine quotes from sources it draws from its memory. Usually, Plato's Net prefers to quote scriptures, and history books, but this time it chooses to speak with the voice of a great African author. It speaks this way to me, cutting through the celebration. The projection is of Chinua Achebe from his book *No Longer at Ease*: "Umuofia would have required of you to fight in her wars and bring home human heads. But those were days of darkness . . . ." The machines speak to me in a voice that they think I'll understand. But they pause to have bouts of static popping and zip-bleeping. They continue to quote Achebe: "Today we send you to bring knowledge . . . ." They spurt out, "Zip. Bleep. Kresh. Pop!" And they continue quoting Achebe: "I have heard of young men from other towns who went to white man's country, but instead of facing their studies they went after the sweet things of the flesh . . . ." The digital re-creation of Achebe freezes momentarily, before saying, "A man who does that is lost to his people. He is like rain wasted in the forest . . . Do not be in a hurry to rush into the pleasures of the world like the young antelope who danced herself lame when the main dance was yet to come."

These zipping and popping currents could make your eyelids peel backward, and as I turn the corner, they get louder. When I'm confronted by a tractor beam of bright lights so bright they must be designed to abduct thoughts, I become limp. They assume the panic has induced yet another coma, but I remain in full control of my body. It's hard to explain, but when, knowingly, you re-enter the otherside, you gain full control over every microscopic nano-fiber of your being.

The mechanical network of machines diagnoses me to better understand if it has been bested. But I don't obey the commands they give to my body. A conscious individual would have to react, but I make sure not to demonstrate consciousness, unlike a child feigning sleep that can be roused by simply tickling them. I act just as I was when I first left normal life. I maintain normal functioning of the respiratory center of my brain to suggest no sign of brain damage, so they test my pupils. They're reacting normally and equally, which

172

suggests that my sudden coma is toxic, and I remain absent in all extra-ocular movements to suggest that I am in a deep coma state.

I start telling myself over and over how I'll fight through the wires, and days go by where I begin to feel my muscles metastasize some, and I feel like a mummy must feel.

The electronic embassy holds onto me. I know now that they think very little of my choices.

I hear them talking about me:

"He could have brought anyone back into Loyd's body for all we know," a human lobbyist tells Plato in front of the council.

Plato says, "He could have chosen a person who was his own blood relative, like the old postman from Woodlawn that wrote poetry that nobody ever read, but instead he brought back a man to whom he isn't even a direct descendant."

They think little of my choice to bring Hank back to life in place of my biological grandfather. If it wasn't bad enough already, that I didn't have Loyd's soul come back to its own body, I could have at least picked a relative or a direct ancestor. Instead I chose to help give my old friend a second chance at living life.

They keep me locked up for days, but they still think I'm unresponsive. During my passing their tests and parsing my time, I find the security measures begin to become lighter around my room. I finally fight through the wires, crawl through the mud, and coat my lungs with cement before I'm finally free. I do what it takes to get to see the light of day, and I tell myself I'll find my way.

But instead I find Hank at Woodlawn Manor, where I had once helped him work on the place. He's there to check on Fifi, but she's asleep.

"I went through a lot to get you here," I say to Hank, "so all you do is look through her window?"

"I don't want to scare her," he says. "She won't recognize me. It was a mistake bringing me back, and you know it. I'm not this guy."

"You made a lot of good decisions," I say. "Look at her. She's here because of you, and so am I."

"What do you know?" Hank says. "You were a boy, and I couldn't even get you to help fix this house into a home. How'm I going to—What do you expect? For me to run this technology? I don't get technology. I'm just a truck driver. I was."

"Hold it high," Hank instructs. "Get that brace away. You don't need it."

The drywall dust settles after the ceiling opens up to let swarms of moonlight arrive inside. My grandmother sees the mess in the dining room after waking on account of all of our noise. The tarp holding the roof of the Manor together looked cleaner before we arrived. Fifi pulls a gun on us because she doesn't know the young guy I'm with and doesn't see me where I stand. I creep out slowly from behind the tarp, and she lowers the weapon when she sees me. She drops the gun altogether, falling to the ground when she sees Hank looking at her through Loyd's eyes. She spasms, like they do in the ether. It's a joyous, freeing dance that her muscles do. Her mind can't comprehend, so her body tremors and trembles, and she shakes free the muscles of a once nimble ballerina.

"It's me, Fifi," says Hank. "It's me, your one-eyed frog." But she's too overcome with confusion.

The event ruins Hank's appetite for harboring emotions from his previous life. He tried to come back to the old Manor and repair things he couldn't get to while he was alive, but he failed.

In a nice, gentle way, I explain to him how he might be able to push Fifi back into an embodiment if we time it right, but Hank insists that she live out the course of her life naturally. "Who knows what will happen when she dies," he says, "that's a different story, you know?" I nod and agree to help him bring her back to life if she dies with unfinished business.

Something happens to a man when he comes back to life. Being charged with life enables the soul to complete even the most insurmountable tasks. Tasks that seemed once insurmountable are no longer as arduous. They're definable.

Loyd walks onto a shipping vessel that rests on the waters in a harbor near Baltimore. It's a vessel being loaded with parts of nocturnal cleaners to bring across the Atlantic. The machines know he's there. They also know he's not really Loyd. But he makes people happy, singing in Italian.

"I'll find out what Italy is all about for myself," says Hank, as he straightens the soybean tie around his neck.

"I bet living in Sicily will be something," I tell him.

"I've been sure all my life, and now I've finally done it. I'm going to find out what it's like to live again."

TWO

Embodiment

Lynch didn't realize it, but I found him too. He was on the otherside longer than my grandfather, but he wasn't awake to what it was about, at least not in the same way that Hank was when I found him. My mother's biological father had left her when she was just a small child, he left her to fend for herself, but she had people to care for her. She eventually became the daughter of the man who had came into her life when he married her mother. They quarreled terribly as my mother was going through her teenage years. Hank treated her badly because he wanted a child of his own, and she got back at him by stealing his motorcycle. Only, he didn't know she stole it, so when the cops caught up with her, who do you think had to bail her out?

"We won't tell Fifi about this one," he said to her after paying her bail. When he came back to life as Loyd, instead of the politician, well . . . . It didn't take long to realize he wouldn't be able to keep focused on political gains. I thought our plan would hold up better and leave Lilloo to me.

It was a horrible mistake bringing him back in place of her fiancé, and I doubt she'll ever love me. How could she love me after how cruel I've become? I planned and reasoned only for myself. I thought he could slip away after making a press conference speech to millions, something they recorded several times. But Loyd didn't look right. He wasn't moving the room the way he once did. He was a man in a suit, who nervously read the cue cards, desperately pining to make a break for a cigarette.

How simple yet horrible it all was!

I now realize the error of my ways, and I'm sorry. Tear me apart. Feed me to the fish while you're out at sea, will you?

As Plato's epigram, *Death at Sea*, reminds me, in this life, I am but a simple sailor, and I have made my grave hoping only to cast some freedom for myself, from the passing ships near my tomb. I am lost.

He's gone again, but he ran off on his own this time. Heaven will have to wait to take him when he ages again, when his time is over once more. They spat him back up and he couldn't handle being back. He ran off like a coward to the ocean, to the sea to learn a new trade. He said he'd learn a new trade and leave everyone alone.

They all knew it wasn't the real Loyd, but they didn't have any way to prove it wasn't really him. They had no way of showing that it wasn't actually Loyd inside, picking up his body and moving it along. Technically speaking, the procedure appeared to have worked. For, the man's body became reanimated. The corpse has come back to life like I came back from the comatose state. Valentine was right when he said it would be no different bringing back a dead man.

The trick to reconstructing my burned body into more than a corpse was a miracle of modern science. I'm able to communicate with limbs that were once lifeless when the muscles contorting the bones were badly burned. Bringing back Hank into his former shell of existence, into his own dead body, would have been an exhaustive trick. Yet, it very well might have worked. For, it worked for Victor Frankenstein. It could have worked again, but I found raising a dead old man's body too complicated. In the meantime, a newly deceased, preserved body awaited, and besides, it was far more convenient to bring Hank back into Loyd's body in place of his own, given the simple reason that within the e-embassy's ELECTRIC ROOM, Valentine's machine had been communicating with Loyd's corpse in order for the embodiment to happen, so it was the only sure way to bring back my old friend, my grandfather.

By focusing on the sensation of returning to sleep, my dreams are full of void and nothingness. After existing on the otherside and returning to life again, I figured it would work in my favor to help give my old friend a second chance at life, for, selfishly, I thought it would free up Lilloo to be all mine when my friend would run off to live in her fiancé's body.

I didn't realize how greed drove my every motive. Yet, to have everything I've desired for so long, I was willing to pay the price.

Loyd died in a way that was not my doing. It was a raid that I would have fought if I were there myself. It was unfortunate, and I would have fought with him to the bitter end, I contend, by his side. But his untimely death shouldn't guarantee his return only for the mere fact that he and his name have a highly regarded status in society.

Well, I was dealing the cards in the game, bringing one lucky soul back to exist on life's side of the coin. I told the one soul I figured I should tell. I told him in the ether, "Focusing on images in the mind's-eye while in the ether, specifically images like those projected to Loyd's body—That's how you take over the body."

"What are you talking about?" Hank had asked me.

"Do you want to come back to life, or should I bring back this shrimp?" I asked the old man. Loyd's soul twitched and he began to spasm with great emotion. The contortion made him into an ejaculatory, sweaty beast, gross and glistening with the stench of being newly dead, after living a life that wasn't truly fulfilled, and he writhed as he watched and felt the pull to the land of the living. He felt the people all around the world talking about his death, and soon he would feel them talking about his reemergence. I had conquered the burden of knowing what existence and non-existence are like, and I offered that to my old friend. At first he denied it.

"I'll just get in the way," he said.

"You'll be able to do anything you wish you would have done while you were living," I said.

So he focused on the soy tie, and through focusing on like images in the mind's-eyes, images being projected to Loyd's mechanically preserved corpse, Hank's soul was ripped from the ether. Through a formless, shapeless existence. In a translucent foggy haze. Embodiment. Like leaving a dream. He immediately experienced panic, unlike the peaceful seizures of entities within the ether.

Lilloo looked to his blinking, blood-red eyes, and she could tell it wasn't her fiancé behind Loyd's lids.

THREE

Understanding the Ether

I f you understand hyper sensitive emotional states brought on by the repetitive nostalgia of watching technology emulate former memories—the fish leaping from its tank—you'll have no trouble grasping its effect on the ether. The ether is busier and less crowded overall. Past ancestors who have been dead for centuries, who had the accomplishment of simply living while being recorded, go back to the living side regularly enough to not get bored with it. Life is tied up and enjoyable, you see. If you can control yourself as a living individual, meaning not getting so wrapped up in the implementation, like Valentine most certainly is, then you have it. You'll have this option to join back to the memories and a system of infinite resources, but of those that turn from machines, seldomly, if ever, do we look back. To be fair, the painful memories become lesser and more distant from one another, for when the machine views the user experiencing an overwhelmingly negative emotion, it is very careful not to make itself unwelcomed.

Therefore technology has inserted itself at the pinnacle of human achievement, and in doing so it became part of governing individuals. The craze of reading social media feeds of politicians and politicianas wore out eventually, when we realized our viewership was what was steering the ship, so we spread the word, talking about it right in front of the childishly brilliant light and sound machines, with their digital image recognizers and sound production capabilities that had been crafted to be sharper than the gusts of a cyclone.

180

"Hey! Those machines you have control of directly feed our reality! You get to watch your fantasy! It's a choose your own adventure story!" The government shutdown was made permanent, as we became reliant on our own viewership to steer the ship called Earth. We realized passing out digital voting machines to everyone was a risk, but the belief was that the good will outweigh the bad because life loves existing. Now, without national barriers, the human being populations throughout the world travel quicker than and freer than any other creature known to exist throughout all time.

Other civilizations on Earth have existed to this extent before though, but those civilizations fell. The technology they used was similar, but they developed theirs to act as machines of war and propaganda. Finally, human and machine are together. Neither has got to fall. For the first time ever, the beings of Earth have combined their love of life with the machine's love of existing. But don't be alarmed when violence erupts. For, we haven't done away with aggression. There's still aggression, but the amount of positive, conscious admiration outweighs anything that comes its way.

I was sent on a simple mission to enter the ether and bring back a man who many believed to possess the words to ease the raids that surrounded our cities. The people living outside the cities aren't all bad, but we must talk to those that are harboring aggression towards progress to try to convince them to see the light, that living in fear of all technology is not necessary. While abandoning it is a choice, the radical mentality to draw forth conviction from another for unifying under the significant reality of a people united against human evolution isn't necessary. Live without it all together, or if you decide to be part of it, either is fine, but don't seek to bring destruction.

We voted and granted to our sibling, the artificial intelligence, the right to kill, to squash or destroy anyone who has a conviction for devastation.

Lilloo thought she was in her final moments of existing when the lunar cleaner, modeled after one of the greatest shopping centers, came to her rescue. It was the greatest place to buy a suit, get a mortgage, have a cup, or watch a hero die.

Loyd was killed by a raider before the health services vessel could arrive. His body was being preserved with Lilloo by his side. And all I needed to do was convince him to refresh his body and mind with the help of a system developed by Valentine, a system he developed as an experiment on the young child I was. I wouldn't be surprised to find out he was behind the fire that brought me to pieces. That fire that caused me to need reconstruction.

After all, that fire caused the chain of events that brought me back from the afterlife, and they wanted to show the entire human species how they were able to bring a guy back to life, thinking that particular medical marvel would stop the raiding.

After the psychic reading was over, I saw him in the audience alright. I saw Loyd there with his hair the way it always stayed put in that neat combed way, without using any products. He looked chipper to see me, as always, but he was quickly overwhelmed like a fish who had landed out of his tank. His body shook rapidly, and he really couldn't communicate well at all, but he wasn't in pain. He was overwhelmed by the feeling of being.

"Those seizures are the best," said my grandfather before Loyd could shake again. And the man went back to work. He was working on something for my grandmother.

I tried to explain, "Grandma is still alive." But he wouldn't listen. He shoved past like I wasn't there.

That's when I took off that stupid, soy-based tie from around Loyd's lumpy throat, and I gave it to my grandfather to hold.

"You want to see your wife again?" I asked him.

"Yeah! Who are you?" he asked. "Oh, will you look who it is! Shane. Good to see you again. Do you have a cigarette?"

He listened with intrigue as I explained to him how he has to come back in place of Loyd if he wants to help his wife again.

"Alright, but I'll need my glasses to see what you're talking about," he said.

"You understand you're dead already."

"Oh," he said, "of course. Just sometimes I forget."

"Well," I said, "Loyd had perfect vision."

"He did?"

"Yep," I said, and I lied a little. This time instead of telling him I was going to be a boxer, I told him he was going to rejoin the living in the body of a baseball player. I said, "He used to pitch for the Birds!"

FOUR

The Suitable Occupation

Mother and I haven't talked much since seeing Hank leave off on a barge with the name FREIGHT SHAKER tattooed on its steel hull. We haven't put too much thought to words between us. After we watched him walk aboard in the body of a young politician, we realized that Hank just might have turned out to be the greatest charlatan of them all, even greater than the foolish character in my poems, those which my ancestral skills had concocted. In his new life, Hank appeared to be as satisfied with living as Loyd as Jay Hedges was with living off a new farm. He was comfortable with the charade, while the real Loyd's soul doth remain quivering the flutters as an entity bound to the ether.

. . .

> *"The groans of tilling*
> *Give Jay an awful feeling,*
> *So Jay Hedges does depart*
> *From home with hope for a new start*
> *With a Beautiful creature,*
> *One he'd never seen before.*
>
> *After meeting Lilly,*
> *Jay wishes to see no more."*
> —*The Hedges*, issue no. 42

. . .

184

Now, Hank lives out his worldly desires, keeping death's mask hidden. In such a way that death's mask does follow, we witnessed Hank wear his costume; 'twas no stranger than watching a colonel at war for the first time. But this time of peace is a pleasant offering for the politician.

"So that's it," she said drearily, and with stinging conceit, after waiting for consensus, she said, "My father is gone again."

"I guess so," I said, and I tried to approach my mother to console her, to give her a hug, but she wants to be left alone to grieve by herself.

"That was my father," she said, "more than anyone else was." She wouldn't let herself show weakness in front of me, so she held back from crying there, until Hank turned on his CB-radio:

"Good to see this old junk still works," said Hank, and he waved to us from the barge. "Arrivederci! Did you hear? Signora Fifi, it's the one-eyed frog—"

"Cut that out," said Fifi, using the CB-radio he left at Woodlawn Manor.

"Keep the front door painted blue, I'll stay on the ocean thinking of you."

While feeling for their moments, I couldn't help but think for a brief period of time, what it would have been like to bring back the biological grandfather, the man I feared I would become, the one I visited in the ether that couldn't even think of my name. I came to a conclusion that the departed poet who left Woodlawn, a poet by the name Sherwood Lynch, would have only stayed around long enough to dust himself off from coming back from the dead when he realized who we were. He would realize who we are, and he'd go off to find the old hag he ran off with when he ran off before.

In my mind, I couldn't help but reel on and on about becoming like Lynch. The thought plagued me, and not just because I felt like I was finding myself taking up a suitable occupation as a poet, but the explicit notion of running away when I someday have children of my own was what I feared most. That horrible feeling might have never left my heart. It could have hardened inside of me, eating away at the love and kindness I had gathered. I might have rotted away that way someday if not for what my mother did say to me that day. She said, "Some people just aren't meant to be fathers. They're not born for it . . . . "

From where we stood on the bridge by the harbor we could hear Hank cursing, like his former self, at the crew onboard. He was yelling about the lack of quality television. "The reception is caput! Do you—Do we have any movies?"

Mother smiled at me, victoriously, and she said, "Some people are."

Sometimes even a simple poet needs his mother to help him remember. For, I was a child who couldn't stop putting his hand on stoves, and swallowing things. Putting remote controls in fish tanks. One time I even burned down my apartment, and I forgot who I was entirely, until mother bopped me on the head. So I suppose she thought she'd help me remember that I still hadn't talked to Lilloo to tell her how I feel.

Mother and I haven't talked since then, for we realized our places in the world are quite different. Strangely, even though we wish all the best for the other, like old friends do, we have different approaches to life. She's the true artist, for she denies her talent only to hide away her beautiful creations. She would have liked to hide me

186

away in my own apartment when Valentine's experiments carried my soul backward from the land of death and sorrow, away from the forgotten affairs.

And if not for Dr. Sonny Valentine, I might still be lost.

My mother's the quiet artist, but I am the outspoken poet, and I must use this so called gift. I must not deny myself the chance to prove to the world how love, and laughter, and whimsy are always around. They are no commodity! They are an abundant, beautiful experience we must always have at our doorstep. Look to the meadows. Listen to the sound of the breeze providing the stalks of wheatgrass with dance. That same thing is alive within you and I. It is alive!

That's when I left to go see the woman I love, and I hope with all my heart that she will understand why I couldn't bring her fiancé's soul back from the ether. It wasn't all done out of cruelty, not done to simply sabotage the man who held the hand of the woman I want to hold.

Regardless, the machines stopped me. I wasn't far from the sea-port. I should have anticipated the grand event being heavily monitored, for even in times of peace, we are all still gearing up to defend against a raid. Our peaceful spirits, and whatever similar substance may evoke peace within the machines helped ease my situation considerably. The artificially intelligent sentinels that picked me up are connected to the larger network that operates in tandem with a human component. As far as peace is concerned, the overall opinion of the public includes peace talks between the borders. It's quite the positive reaction, and it's a reaction to Hank's speech. In the end, neither man nor machine could fully comprehend what it must have been like in the ether. They couldn't grasp it, and the man in the paisley robes who observed my dilemma had stepped down from summoning spirits, so they made no further attempt to control the ether. But they understand what it must be like to land somewhere and not be able to immediately return, like Loyd's soul might still hang on the edge of understanding his fate in that awful brink of confusion.

The sentinels and democratic human authority have come to a census to allow me to go back into society, but they're confused. Despite my contributions in creating what may very well be a temporary peace for all humanity, a guy like me doesn't fit in so easily among zips and blasts of electric circuits and circuitry. The light-emitting panels mean nothing to me. All I have are words, and I'm drowning in their euphemisms.

"You better slow down, big guy," says a human recruiter accompanying the sentinels.

"I'm a maverick, man," I tell him. He laughs uproariously as I shout, "You can't hold me back." I extend an arm to introduce myself. "I won't be able to find a place worth resting, will I?"

"You should be grateful," says a robotic sentinel. "You've contributed to soul-loss of one of our greatest human relations. Loyd was bred to-to talk to us, with his word-words, like you. But yours was a failed experiment."

"If I am a failed abomination, why have you not destroyed me where I stand?"

"It would be a waste," says the cyborg. "None among the living, nor among the robotic, have understandings of the world of the dead. Not like you."

"Then I must write verse to unite and bring peace."

"You will bring peace with your words alright," says the cyborg, with an apparent understanding of sarcasm. Upon their orders, I am ushered away to take a peaceful suitability test. The test is fifty questions, designed to gauge my personality. They find that I'm on track in most of the groups of questions, meaning I'm comfortable taking some risks, I'm capable of interacting with others, my style of decision making is desirable, I have the desired attitude towards authority, and I exude other optimal personality traits as well.

As the testing for suitable peacekeeping occupations is now complete, I await the results without enthusiasm in an office with vertical blinds that let a little light into the bleak space. After realizing I'm not a threat to the paradigm, the recruiters inform me that they've formed a unanimous decision. They've decided to move me towards employment within the civil services sector of society, as a police officer.

FIVE

Reformed

"No matter how dramatically democratic our reforms are, or how smooth human and machine relations become, the role of the peacekeeper will never be forgotten."
—Electronic Embassy Recruiter

Initially, they were pressing me to join their ranks as a peacekeeper more than I could have ever anticipated. I was surprised they actually wanted my judgmental workings to play a part in shaping my community, so I asked them about their reasoning. I asked the human recruiter, with his silvery flat-top cut; I asked, "What makes you think I'm a good fit to keep order after I disobeyed orders?"

The recruiter thought for a moment, with his hands folded on his belly, leaning back in his chair. His plaid shirt, with its thin, crossing lines looked like a chain-link fence. I wondered if children ever came up to hit his protruding ribcage to see if his type of acorns fall down, and I wondered what the wise oak would do to keep peace in such a wild scenario. "You did what you felt was right," he said to me. "We can't always follow orders. It seemed greedy at first, which is why we hunted your ass, but you doing what was right for you turned out to be right for all of us."

"So that makes me holier than most," I torted.

"Not at all," he told me, which eased my mind greatly to know the man wasn't at liberty to feed my ego at whichever degree I requested. "You're able to make mistakes. We all are, Shane. But your

190

empathy and understanding, towards other ethnic backgrounds, as observed through the Valentine Experiments—You're familiar, right?"

"Of course I am," I said snobbishly.

"Oh, well, great," he said. "Well, your understanding of such characteristics in human form mixed with your understanding of life, and death, not to mention your nature of writing things down, poetically—"

"Stop," said I, sensing him pandering at last.

"Yes, of course," he said, "well, you see, these things make you an ideal candidate for keeping peace in Woodlawn."

I thanked him, and I told the recruiter how I'd have to graciously decline the very kind offer. "I'll remain a poet," I said. "Living where I'd like. To bring joy to others. And I'll live off the fruit of the lands too.

"I'm smart enough not to do anything stupid to get a quick dollar, hard-working enough not to starve, and creative enough to climb from the ashes yet again," I said.

"Very well," said he. We shook hands. "I admire your vocation," he told me before we parted ways, and I went off looking for the woman I want to love eternally if she'll allow it.

It's my chance to cast my treasured heart before my dearest desire, to throw my apple before her, and I will see what type of love she has for me, for I wish to ravish her beauty while it remains, and while I remain steadfast in her memories.

Locating Lilloo isn't an easy task. She stopped using any means of contacting the outside world after her father died at the hands of human hatred. She feels that technology will lead to more bloodshed, that it promotes the pointless, arbitrary toil of the inescapable meandering of the human spirit. She opposes ideals that are constantly voted on and reformed. It's as if humanity has found a way to smooth out the clay form that a hurrying god or goddess had sloppily put together. We, the creation, created our own Adam too, and now we rejoice by plugging a democratic voting mechanism in the hand of any adult who wants to take part.

They're figuring out the world problems, distributing wealth and resources among everyone as fairly as the system can evolve to permit. We're being aided by the creation once more. They clean the air we breathe, they grow the food we eat, and they help us unify with each other. Our creation is alive now more than ever. Valentine fought to bring this type of realization about—and he fought knowing full well he'd leave the living forever—still, Lilloo wants no part of it.

How could she? She saw those ideals clash with an antithesis that did take from her everyone she loved, and now she's left alone to define what it means to be alive. But I've found her, lurking in the one place no man or machine will dare to enter. Ever since the major religions started using the electronic political process to reform their ways of practice and worship, the old buildings have become boarded up, condemned shells of their former selves.

The equal distribution of wealth meant less distribution of canned goods, and fewer homeless types need assistance. Religion today is more personal than ever, yet beliefs differ as they always have. The majority of religious buildings have been converted to shopping centers, housing, space for public performance, or—in the case of Lilloo's church—boarded up and left to rot.

She clutches a necklace of broken rosary beads in her closed fist. I'm slow to approach her because I want to offer her the peaceful discussion I hope she's here after.

"It's worse than you think," she says.

"I'm sure it hurts," I tell her, "but it'll get better."

"I've had some news since before I saw Loyd get back up," she says. "And I know that wasn't really him . . . ."

"You're right," I say. "It wasn't really him inside."

"I found out . . . something," she says. "It was an accident, but I don't want to raise this baby alone."

"That might be the best kind of accident," I say, and I tell her I'll help her.

"We agreed," she says, "not to bring a child into this world. It would feel funny to have Loyd's baby after he died. We agreed that this planet is too crowded as it is. I can't raise it now."

I want to scrape from her insides that growing remnant of her former lover, but as the only act I might try to do with some credence of dignity, the entire time you've known my tale, I say, to her, "I'd like to help you raise the child of another man as my own child."

She puts away the rosary and stands to say to me, in a deafening tone, "I don't know if I want that . . . ."

SIX

Farewell Address

My darlings, I wish that I could say that I awoke permanently from dreams, from the ether, from death, but I am still waking. I can't shake the miserable feeling that this life in all its splendorous, whimsical turns and narrow, endless corridors—those that run each of us ragged, like mice racing through mazes for the benefit of science—I can't shake the feeling that this life is but a dream, and I'm back to square one, feeling small and unaware. I begin to feel that it has all been a test. That we, or perhaps just me, are being watched by an observant eye in the sky that records every reaction to stimulus. Or, it could be that another gifted scientist has another Valentine Experiment going on. It could even be the feeling of being watched from the land of death.

After all, our ancestors and our loved ones need something to keep them entertained for all eternity. Loyd surely spasmed something extra when Lilloo spoke about their agreement, and when I left her to make her own decisions, surely those spirits on the otherside shifted while watching our faces intertwine and unwind, like chimes hanging in the air after a wind storm ceases to blow, and we settle. We're still connected to the great eternal universe, still suspended on the same Calder mechanisms, but we don't share the same strings. And as we unwind, we separate finely, ready to get twisted in a different contortion. Oh! Constant twisting. When will we be set free?

In time, the unknown will all be known. Truth looms in the distance, taunting each of us with its tongue drawn out between its teeth, like a child, but this truth of the unknown that we yearn for is all that has ever lived and died. Ancient ancestors, and societies lost forever watch together. They watch us and taunt us to come closer to death, and sometimes they'll push us to grow in life.

Love grows if you nourish it. A child does grow if you let it be born. Of course plants do grow too, with water and sunlight; see how the simple, green Earth is easier to tend to? This is why the trees don't fight and cry the way that humanity does. The raiders destroyed each other. They took people's lives, burned down forests, and plucked giant machines from the clouds to fill their unsettled minds. Man's ideals will always be paid in blood, but the simple, green plants that grow from the ground only know love.

My feet have found their way from the eastern shore, away from Woodlawn, and they're out of shoes, and socks too. I plant myself on the fields and walk along the soils, outside of those areas where machines fly in the skies. There haven't been any raiders in the endless jungles. Just the old-fashioned dangers of being bit by snakes, or speared by fellow fishing tribes. That's all the excitement I need anymore.

The farmers plow the fields here, and because there's no real pollution in the tiny villages I visit, they will always be in charge of their fields.

Let the rest of the world heal itself. I've brought humanity closer to living peacefully with the machines they've created. The flying, carbon-neutral buzzards that have been created in the image of our most prized monuments and buildings will clean the air. The atmosphere of our cities is being returned to the way it once was, before autos and planes filled our lungs with dirt and odorless poisons. I've done my part in helping bring this change about, so now I'll wander where I please. Leave me be, and I'll take part once more if things get out of control. I'm sure they will unravel, but for now let's not get carried away with such frivolous emptiness.

The farmers dance when rain is needed, and today I'll join them on the bare Earth. The soils coat my feet and toes nicely. The dry dirt has been here longer than I, and such dirt will welcome me back into its clutches when my time is up for good. That's for certain. For now, we'll take light steps to bring water down to meet the horizon. With great big gestures of arms high above our heads, and while joining hands, I'm accepted by the farmers and their community, none of which know who I am already. All those people around the world with a screen to point and judge me, and be entertained by my poetry, entertained by 'The Hedges', they live in private homes where they live private lives without ever having to accept me in this way.

Finally, this poet who was asleep in death's bed, I, who felt the Earthly fires turn my skin to rubber, I, who returned to the land of death, I, who communed with my lost relative, I, who feared becoming just like a wicked man who left his family—I have been found. Fear not, humanity! I'll watch with you still. For, though I am no longer lost as I was, I will not let people lose themselves again.

It's poetry. It doesn't have to be complicated, riddled with pretentious words and rhymes. It keeps people fed on thought. It keeps them humble and thinking always. It keeps me thinking. This poetry. It keeps me linking arms with others. Together we look to make our ballads better.

Rambling & meandering onward,
—*S. Sullivan*

. . .

The End

. . . .

A Satyr with The Lost Poet:

" Leaving the Ether "

Dramatis Personae

SHANE SULLIVAN, a poet

SHAUN VAIN, a writer

KING WENSILSLAUS, a king

DIONYSUS, a god

APHRODITE, a goddess

THE QUEEN

THE BOY

COOK

A MINSTREL

A PEASANT

THE PEON

ELIJAH, a gentleman

LEAVING THE ETHER

(Playwriting is the means in which I choose to commune with this muse who is SHANE SULLIVAN. Our only conversations happen adrift, in the same ether from which souls stay for however long. The exploration of however long they stay is the concern of each character in this satyr play.)

SULLIVAN: If they quit looking at holy books, this place would be filled with more strange than I could handle.

SHAUN: Have you found religions get along well in this place?

SULLIVAN: There's no struggle for land or territorial quarreling if that's what you mean.

AUN: I do believe that's what I mean.

SULLIVAN: Well when feuds erupt it's because one entity will be jealous of another entity being pulled from the ether more than they. Oh! There's a riot over yonder.

AUN: Let's listen.

SULLIVAN: Do.

(From over heaps of spasmatics—the quivering piles of mind-glue that have joined the afterlife without comprehension, as usual—comes the trumpets of one king, Wensilslaus, who is confused over why the god he fought to promote isn't allowing his departure from the ether.)

KING: You'll pardon me never. If you find the claws of death wrap round your throat once more, and if you haven't already brought the choirs to chant my name above the organ's groan, you'll find a strict dismissal of your religion from our kingdoms.

DIONYSUS: What will you do to error my ways? My vessel is eternally afloat. The minds of my disciples call me to an Earthly arena on a regular basis. Don't threaten me, or else I'll wreck your kingdom with fire or wave, or I'll bring a wind so cold it will freeze their hearts.

KING: You'll do that? You'll kill your believers to keep me from returning to my lands?

DIONYSUS: They'll believe me even more. Anyone left after the disaster will call on me for their protection.

KING: What if I have my people look to a new deity, what then?

DIONYSUS: Your sheep won't stray.

KING: Let me try.

APHRODITE: If his people stray to me, I'll promise they won't have to eat soup from rusted cans.

KING: They like soup.

APHRODITE: But the cans are rusted and made of lead.

KING: They like soup though. Very much. Let's watch.

(The KING's people are at a table. THE QUEEN is dressed in a beautiful gown. She looks stunning in the court of paupers.

THE BOY ladles out soup to the people.)

A PEASANT: My soup is cold. I'll add hot water to cool it less. Say boy, bring me hot water, will you?

(THE BOY goes to the COOK.)

COOK: I won't stand for it! Adding hot water to cooled soup. It's gazpacho! It's a chilled soup for a reason!

(The COOK goes to the group eating.)

COOK: Where is the fool?

(THE BOY brings over A MINSTREL.)

COOK: Not-a him! Ah! Where is the son or daughter of a bitch-a? Ah! Who didn't like cooled gazpacho?

(A PEASANT steps forward.)

A PEASANT: It was me. I'd rather die than eat this gruel. Bring me a better soup.

(The next day, A PEASANT is having lunch with THE PEON at a better place to eat.)

THE PEON: What is the soup of the day?

WAITER: We'll put yesterday's vegetables that no one ate along with butts of meat in a hot pot filled with water, broth, and other bloods of the earth.

205

A PEASANT: I'll have that too.

KING: Do you see? You must understand how, in my kingdom, the kindness of the heavens is measured not in gold, nor fancy clothing. Everyone is content as long as he or she is able to find the soup he or she desires.

APHRODITE: That's explicit enough for me. I'll have a go at it.

(*APHRODITE dives into the kingdom, but she is thrown back.*)

APHRODITE: They think my soups are too spicy!

SULLIVAN: Don't get caught up in that riot. Going back to the living from the land of the dead is enjoyable, though.

(*In the land of the living on Earth, ELIJAH reads SULLIVAN's poetry aloud, and suddenly SULLIVAN is there with him. He plays a trick on ELIJAH by fogging up the mirror in his flat, and writing, "Look Behind You," in the foggy glass, but the Englishman is preoccupied with something he's reading about THE POET. When he's finished reading, SULLIVAN returns to the otherside.*)

THE WRITER: I'm content only leaving when I'm really needed.

THE POET: Oh, so that's why you self-publish, eh?

SHAUN: That's the life of a starving artist. To write until we can't write any longer, and publish it on our own because we can, and we can stand a chance of getting our ideas out there. I'll have no role in amping up my persona. I'm no longer interested in appearing for the sake of novelty, because there's something more important at stake.

SULLIVAN: It's freeing. It's rather wild and untamed. You've let people look into your mind. That's for sure. I, and all of this, we are your vision of . . .

AUN: Thank you, Shane. But I'll be on my way.

SULLIVAN: You will be? Oh, but you've just arrived. You can't leave already. We're just getting started. I'm your monster to be met.

:   Yes, thank you for being him, and I, I am needed to write something new. Do you understand?

SULLIVAN: Do.

THE END.

Get ready for a

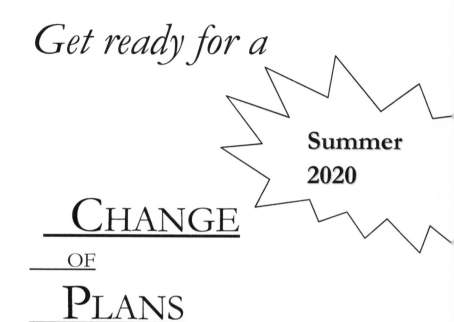

Summer 2020

CHANGE
OF
PLANS

"Two books from . . .

. . . Sonny Valentine."

. . . . THE BALLAD AND FOUR GIANTS . . . .

also known as *The Ballad of Andre Thespies and the Four Giants of the Modern World*

—Full text coming Winter 2019—

Our words aren't our own before they leap from lips. Before a sound is uttered, those *oo*'s and *ha*'s belong to another kind of creature. Hardly human and technically not alive any longer, the creature in this revolutionary tale was once very much alive— and during that instance he was technically a person while he was alive, too— yet, Aesop hides like a creature behind the curtain of all tales. Moreover, Aesop's entire world lives behind our tales.

This story presented here has been given to a man known all over as Andre Thespies. It arrived in his possession in another form written by the wife of Aesop, and I declare with grateful humility, and humble gratitude, what drives this show is from stories of Aesop's and Sally's incarnation.

But what worth is there for me to know where from, forthwith, doth perchance reckoning all creation? I'll tell you what it's worth to scrub the literary prowess from the stained teeth of scholars who've lectured it to death, but I'll make it sing to you in a new way on the stage of a page.

The lights shut off all at once with a surge of electricity and pulsating sounds fill the space. Andre Thespies, better known as Paul, is a playwright with a following in his hometown. Despite sold-out performances of his Off-Broadway shows, Paul hasn't found the love he deserves and he feels his plays are underwhelming audiences. They speak of society as a band of brothers and sisters united in causes, but their causes are speckled with sophisticated dilemmas, which make up the basis of plots he writes. Knights find romance but fear the disease of fighting for a particular regime. Lovers are parted by bloodshed, and matrimony is tested by swooners that step in when husbands are at war.

—EXCERPT—

Andre hasn't lived a real life yet because he's been too busy pumping his fictional tales full of the melancholy portrayals of drama coupled by the lives of people from his life, most of which never gave a damn about him to begin with, until his plays did well.

Here's a scene now:

Outside of a broken-down, old rambler of a sports utility style of vehicle stands a pale-faced guard. The man with a bald head looks injured. He takes off his guard's jacket, and he reveals a long gash on his shoulder. Dyanna passes him a towel from the glove compartment to use as a bandage until he can find better care. He spits on the towel before smearing the sticky saliva onto his hairy skin to remove some of the dried blood from himself.

"This hurts a bitch."

"It hurts a what?" asks Dyanna. "You know, I know you're in pain, but you can't talk like that."

"I'd better get another hobby then," says Stephen.

"You should know better than to shoot at skeet in the morning before roll call. Everyone seeing us together thinks I like your cheesy fingers touching my door like that."

Steven quits holding onto Dyanna's door the way he thought he could lean for support after noticing the marks of fingerprints he laid on her glass window. He huffs on the window to wet it enough to remove smudges from them with his long jacket sleeve.

"You can't get mad at that," says Steven. "Everyone has fingerprints. You know a cop leaves them on your vehicle on purpose."

"Why is that?" asks Dyanna.

"Hey Antonio! Long time, stranger." Antonio passes near the bushes and benches that sit on bricks above a small stream that flows past the college campus and in through the town.

Further down the road is the town of Birkwood and the harbor place with its piers, yachts, and bars where the rocket pilots hang out. Antonio walks to the edge of the path to meet the blacktop, and turns before crossing the lot to say to them, "You're here early today. Are you trying to impress the bosses?"

Steven hurries behind him along the path, saying, "Wait up McCoole," and Dyanna complains, "You're supposed to look at my engine, Steve."

—EXCERPT—

You are formally invited.

FROM THE DESK OF Elijah Wellington Esquire

Coming

Winter 2023

a novel by Shaun Vain

.... ACKNOWLEDGEMENTS ....

To Lady J. G., for holding on while I realized the path of this poet.

To my grandfather, Mel, for not being afraid to tell stories. We never talked about how he wasn't my mother's biological father, but that surely played an influence on this. For the sake of balance, thank you to my biological father for sticking around.

Thanks to everyone I've ever felt as close to as family for supporting my mannerisms. Thank you Ken, for reminding me not to listen to everything I hear on television. Special thanks to my mother, for giving me the entire moon. To my bubbie, for never discouraging me from playing golf in her backyard. To my great-grandmother, for the gift of stories about New Zealand, and for being loving to everyone she's ever met. To my cousins, seeing you grow has been rewarding. To my aunts, for all the horseback rides and talk about butterflies.

Thanks to Future Publishing Service, especially to Flo, for line edits and working with my difficult creative choices, but "Good wins out in the end." Thanks to Julia for proofreading, to Gordon, for pulling me from rivers of white space on the page, thank you to Jack Sr., for digging me from the sandy pit of writer's block. Thank you to everyone at FPS for your hard work. And thank you LaVerne, for making a rhyme better with time.

To my friends, Andrew, Matt, Angela, Sean, Siarra, Bobby, Sid, Joe, Fiona, Jesse, Clint, Freddy, Barbara, and Josh, for helping me sort through ideas, and a special thanks to Umar, for preparing me for the worst, while humbly showing me the importance of bringing forth artifacts.

To David in Point Arena, for your works as a peace-maker, and to the brilliant English professor, Ellen. Thank you D. Reische, for your work navigating current mining issues. Thank you Brian and Koller, for helping me realize that new technology doesn't have to be evil.

Thank you to teachers who've inspired me, especially Kerri, for trusting me to grade her papers, to Irvine and Watson, for thoughts about poetry and philosophy, Mohler, for instilling that I would be someone someday, to Jen, for looking over early drafts. Thank you to Ewa, for inspiring me with your research skills. To all the librarians, scholars, experts, and Holly, for her equestrian knowledge. To researchers, museum staff, like the kindness of Melissa and Steve, scholarly incidents with Shane and Derek, and even Rob. Thank you to all those who have helped me with researching poetry, and philosophy; I'll have another look later.

To Shirley, and Mary, for their talents making images to support my early creations. Thanks to Zbigniew, for unknowingly providing machines for creative works.

To all the poets and writers I've met. Thanks to Wellesley College, for celebrating the National Poetry Month, and to Wesleyan for discussion about ancient plays, and to all the responses I've received to my inquiries. Special thank you to Fishbein, Staten, Mobley, and all others who wrote and published fine stories before I gave a shot. I might not have done this without the examples set forth by you.

I'm grateful for the warm welcome from the art & theatre communities. To theatre spaces, for allowing me room to grow as a storyteller. Thanks to all the film crews for putting up with my scripts. Special thanks to Tony. Thanks to CCBC, Freundel & Horning, UMBC, Kriezenbeck & Salkind, Glass Mind Theatre, friends at the Fringe, and my new fringe friend Bremner. Special thank you to Alexander Scally & Caitlyn Bouxsein, for, creating David Mark Davids as a stage performance inspired a parody (*TLPOW's* Mark David Marks is based on notes from subsequent live performances).

Without going on forever, there are, undeniably, other (countless) impressions made on every writer (and individual). If you've understood some of the ideas in this book, then you might also understand that it's not possible to thank all the people who have had significant undeniable poetic influence upon this work . . .

. . . Thank you for your support!

.... RECOMMENDED READINGS ....

Some quotations were used to assemble this work, including actual quotes taken from several of the following sources, and some sources are included here due to their tremendous influence.

Epigrams by Plato and Praxilla, found in *Greek Lyric Poetry* translated by Willis Barnstone, published by Bantam Books, New York (1962).

Dialogue On Poetry And Literary Aphorisms by Friedrich Schlegel, translated by Ernst Behler and Roman Struc, published by Penn State University Press in University Park, Pennsylvania (1980).

Fragment On Reform by Percy Bysshe Shelley, found in *Percy Bysshe Shelley: Selected Poetry and Prose*, published by Rinehart & Company in New York (1958).

Frankenstein by Mary Shelley, published by Barnes & Noble in New York (2012).

Hyperion by Friedrich Hölderlin, published by Archipelago Books in New York (2008).

Kierkegaard's Philosophy: Self-Deception and Cowardice in the Present Age by John D. Mullen, published by Meridian Books in New York(1981).

La Vita Nuova (Poems of Youth) by Dante Alighieri, published by Penguin Books in London (1969).

No Longer At Ease by Chinua Achebe, published by Fawcett in New York (1960).

The Oresteia by Aeschylus, consisting of *Agamemnon* translated by Richard Lattimore and *Prometheus Bound* translated by David Greene, found in *Greek Tragedies: Volume 1*, published by The University of Chicago Press in Chicago (1991).

. . . .

THE Lost Poet

of Woodlawn

by Shaun Michael Vain

BIOGRAPHY

for Writer/Creator of

*The Lost Poet of
Woodlawn,*

*The Procurements of Sonny
Valentine*

Asleep in the Skies

. . . .

SHAUN VAIN lives in America
but travels and writes fiction
throughout the world.

He loves animals and cycling, and
he's a naturalist.